000003033210

Montana Bound

Cowboys Marty and Harvey, at the end of a trail drive, decide to explore Montana, but fall foul of Jason Thorpe, a bank robber masquerading as a town marshal. In revenge the two cowboys take a gold watch from him but, unbeknown to them, the watch links Thorpe to a Civil War murder – and the killer is determined to get it back.

Marty and Harvey soon become caught up in fighting between Thorpe and his former gang members over stolen bank money. And if Thorpe has his way, they will see Boot Hill before they see Montana.

Montana Bound

Greg Mitchell

A Black Horse Western

ROBERT HALE

© Greg Mitchell 2019
First published in Great Britain 2019

ISBN 978-0-7198-3035-8

The Crowood Press
The Stable Block
Crowood Lane
Ramsbury
Marlborough
Wiltshire SN8 2HR

www.bhwesterns.com

Robert Hale is an imprint
of The Crowood Press

The right of Greg Mitchell to be identified as
author of this work has been asserted by him
in accordance with the Copyright, Designs and
Patents Act 1988

CHAPTER 1

It was strange without the cattle. For nearly three months Harry Paulson and his trail crew had watched the wild Texas longhorns day and night as the herd moved steadily north to the rail head at Abilene.

There had been stampedes, long dry stages and numerous river crossings. Added to these problems were threats from would-be herd-cutters attempting to steal any cattle bearing blotched or unfamiliar brands. Passing through Indian Territory they were harassed by tribesmen demanding tolls. Only demonstrations of a willingness to fight had deterred various human predators waiting to exploit the first signs of weakness.

The drovers had all longed for the day when the cattle had been shipped and they could at last enjoy undisturbed sleep.

With the cattle train loaded, Paulson took his men to the nearest saloon and bought drinks all round. He gave each man a ten-dollar advance on pay and arranged a final settlement at the outfit's wagons the following day. Drunk or sober, they had to be there because the operating plant would be sold and the men needed to collect their personal belongings and firearms.

The marshal in Abilene, one James Butler Hickok, had banned the carrying of guns in the town. More than one trail herder with a skinful of unaccustomed liquor would challenge that rule but Paulson tried hard to keep his crew out of trouble. He would explain that his concern for his men was due to a slight eccentricity: he just hated to hear the wind whistling through bullet holes in his employees.

Marty Redmond and Harvey Collins were the two who seemed least likely to land in trouble. Both were young men who had worked together on the same ranch before signing up for the long drive to Kansas.

Marty was of average height with untidy, dark-brown hair that badly needed cutting. He was lean and soft-spoken. Around horses and cattle, his calm, non-threatening manner was a great asset.

Harvey was taller, well over six feet, even leaner than Marty. He had long sandy hair and sported a drooping moustache. Less reticent than his partner, he would offer his often irreverent but common-sense opinions in a raucous voice when he felt that someone should speak up.

Even for men who had been months on the trail the diversions of Abilene were limited. There were dance-hall girls, drinking and gambling, but all entertainments were designed to separate newly paid cowboys from their money.

Marty and Harvey saw the sights after treating themselves to baths, shaves and haircuts, good meals and a few drinks before they returned to spend a restful night on the ground beside the chuck wagon. No more night-guard misery, trying to stay awake and singing for hours to nervous cattle. The following afternoon they had a proposition to put to Paulson.

The outfit was to be sold up; as well as their wages the drovers were to be given an amount to cover transport expenses to their home bases. But, with bad cases of itchy feet, Harvey and Marty were not going home.

The next day with their badly hung-over companions they lined up for their final pay. Paulson was happy to sell the pair the pick of the remuda at nominal prices before disposing of the rest in Abilene. Knowing that the horses that had served the outfit so well would be in good hands, the trail boss was happy to sell the two men their choices at five dollars per head. He had even suggested to Marty that he should take Lonesome, the fine bay gelding that had been his favourite. The horse walked so quickly that the cowboys always joked that Paulson would get lonesome so far ahead of the others.

Harvey's choice was a tall black mare called Emma. Nobody knew where the name came from and, because of her cantankerous nature, she was often called by more descriptive but less friendly titles. Harvey had ridden the mare regularly and knew her ability. He was not worried about Emma's disposition. He wanted a good horse, not a wife.

The pair decided they would like to see Wyoming or Montana and set about equipping themselves for the journey.

They were careful with their money, seeing no sense in squandering it in Abilene's saloons. Aware that unexpected happenings could bring their plans undone, they did their best to anticipate future difficulties. They had replaced their worn-out clothing and invested in basic camping equipment together with a light tent. A mule and pack-saddle were their next acquisitions so that their riding horses should not be overloaded.

Harvey already owned a Henry rifle and Marty bought a Winchester carbine that took the same .44 ammunition. A gun trader in town bought the old Colt percussion revolvers that they had inherited from various Civil War relatives and Harvey did a deal for a brand-new Smith & Wesson, top-break revolver chambered for the .44 Henry cartridge. Only a few of these were made so Marty had to be content with a converted, open-top Colt that also used the .44

7

rimfire loads. For a few dollars more they were able to buy a couple of second-hand but serviceable cartridge belts and holsters. Each of them bought two fifty-round boxes of ammunition.

'I hope you boys aren't planning to shoot up the town or do something rash like that,' the dealer said, laughing. He could afford to be jocular as business had been a bit slack until the two young cowhands with money in their pockets walked through the door.

'We might need this artillery as we go further west,' Marty had explained. 'Stories are that the Indians are acting up again and folks say there are plenty of road agents along the trail.'

'It might be safer than around here,' the dealer told them. 'Even with Wild Bill Hickok keeping things a bit quieter, there's still far too much shooting.'

'The quieter the better,' Harvey said. 'Months on the trail with fifteen hundred crazy longhorns have given me a distinct dislike of excitement.'

Joe Starkey, the storekeeper, ran a hand through his thinning grey hair and watched his customers depart. If newspaper reports were right about happenings in Montana, he knew that there could be lively times on the trail. All the elements were there: restless Indians, gold, and raw frontier towns, not to mention new ranches opening up. If those boys were sincere in their intentions to avoid excitement Montana was a poor choice.

CHAPTER 2

Their route lay along the north fork of the Platte. They were about to leave their overnight camp when trouble found them.

Their animals were saddled and Harvey was making final adjustments to the mule's pack. Marty had already mounted when a group of riders suddenly appeared over the crest of a nearby ridge.

The newcomers briefly checked their horses, sighted Marty and Harvey and turned their mounts towards them.

Marty heard the shot, 200 yards away, a split second before he heard the sound of the heavy slug striking flesh. Shocked and momentarily confused, he called to his partner as their loaded mule grunted and fell to its knees.

'Basil's hit! Those sonsofbitches are shooting at us.'

Harvey needed no warning as he was standing beside the stricken animal. Later he would thank his lucky stars that his tall frame was thin enough to present a difficult target. His first notion was to grab the Henry rifle from his saddle and fire back at the shooter but a shout from Marty changed his mind.

'Get mounted, Harvey. There's too many of them – leave the pack.'

Another bullet buzzed past the tall cowboy's ear as he snatched up his reins and threw himself into the saddle.

The black mare was in full stride by the time he had managed to pick up both stirrups.

Like many young men raised on the frontiers of Texas, both had been under fire before from Indian raiders or criminals of several types. Consequently they did not flee as blindly as they seemed to be doing.

Marty steadied Lonesome until his partner came level with him, then he shouted: 'Make for that clump of boulders up ahead. We can stand them off and they'll have to cross open ground to get near us. Watch out for prairie-dog holes. There's a few scattered among the sagebrush.'

Both the horses were range-raised and they too were aware of the hazards connected with such country. After chasing stampeding cattle at night they were hardly challenged by daylight gallops. Sometimes they swerved or jumped low obstacles concealed by the sage but gradually they increased their lead.

When the two riders dared take their gaze off the ground ahead they risked quick glances behind. At least half a dozen men were spurring in pursuit but Marty and Harvey were heartened to see that their hunters were falling behind. Neither regretted their decision to buy the best two horses in Paulson's remuda.

Anger swiftly replaced their alarm at the unprovoked attack. Their horses could outrun the pursuers but both men knew the danger of being hit by a lucky shot. The option of discouraging their hunters suddenly had great appeal.

'Let's throw a couple of shots into them – see if they like it,' Marty called as they neared the rocks.

'A good idea,' Harvey agreed enthusiastically.

They rounded a large boulder, halted and stepped down from their saddles. Then each drew his rifle and threw down the reins so that their well-trained horses would stand. By the time they reached firing positions the pursuers were barely fifty yards away.

A grey horse, its sweaty hide caked in red dirt, was struggling to its feet: an obvious victim of a hole in the ground. There was no sign of its rider and Marty and Harvey had no time to look for him.

The foremost pursuer, suddenly confronted by two riflemen, belatedly started hauling on his reins to turn away. Almost casually Harvey knocked him from his horse with his first shot.

A cloud of dust rolled around them as the oncoming riders sat their horses back on their haunches, then wheeled them away.

Marty threw a shot into them as they bunched together and heard a cry of pain. Through the drifting dust he saw a rider slumped in his saddle, clinging to the saddle horn. His horse, with no direction from the rider, turned and followed the others in retreat.

'They're running.' Harvey laughed as he levered another round into his rifle's firing chamber. 'I'll send a few more shots just to hurry 'em along.'

'Forget about them, Harvey. That coyote you shot is lying out there in the sagebrush. He might still be able to shoot and so could the rider who was on that grey horse when it fell. Keep an eye out in case the others decide to come back and I'll see if I can find those two.'

Harvey agreed. After warning his friend to be careful he set his rifle sight for long range and focused on the small group of riders who had halted at their old campsite about half a mile away. The distance was far too much for accurate shooting but the elevated rear sight was set to catch anyone who came into effective range as he approached.

Marty slipped another couple of rounds through his carbine's loading port. Crouching low, he ran to a slightly higher point from where he could see down into the sage. From there he could discern the man Harvey had shot. He

11

was lying crumpled in an awkward manner that no conscious man would adopt and a dark pool of blood was visible near his head.

Satisfied that Harvey's victim was no longer a threat, Marty looked around to where the grey horse was standing on three legs. Something black but dusty was showing through a gap between two low-growing sage bushes. The morning sun was just high enough to glint on metal near by: probably a gun of some sort. Marty sighted carefully along the barrel of his Winchester.

'You in the brush,' he called, 'put your hands up and stand up. Be quick about it.'

The bushes shook violently and a pair of hands emerged, then a head.

'No tricks, or you're dead,' Marty warned as a big man, his black suit covered in red dust, struggled clumsily to his feet.

He was middle-aged, with a neatly trimmed moustache under a crooked nose that must once have been badly broken. Greying hair showed beneath his black hat. His face bore a worried expression which was quickly replaced by a defiant glare.

'Who are you?' Marty demanded.

'I'm a special marshal,' the man replied. 'My name's Jason Thorpe and the men with me are a legally authorized posse, for all the good they've been. But I reckon you would already have suspected who I am.'

'Keep your hands up. I don't care who the hell you are. I'll shoot you if you make one wrong move. Where's your gun?'

'There's one lying at my feet and one dropped out of the holster when my horse fell. There's a Spencer carbine on my saddle.'

'Move a bit closer but keep your hands up. I'm mighty anxious to know what brought on this downright unfriendly

12

action of yours.'

'The bank at Cedar Flat was robbed a couple of days ago and you two fit the robbers' descriptions,' Thorpe explained.

'What descriptions?' Marty demanded suspiciously.

'There were two of them, one a tall skinny character riding a black horse, and the other around normal height and riding a bay horse. Both were said to be young – about your ages.'

'So you decided to kill us just on that vague description?'

'One of my men got carried away,' Thorpe replied dismissively. 'You know that citizens deputized from small towns are not always the best material for this work. But he paid the price for it. That's him lying over there.'

'And I suppose your horses just bolted towards us?'

'You ran.'

'And we're mighty dammed lucky that we did. You were prepared to shoot us on sight. We are not bank robbers and we don't even know where Cedar Flat is.'

'It sounds as though there might be a misunderstanding,' Thorpe said smoothly. 'Come in with us and we can try to fix this mess.'

'I'm not that dumb. We don't know who you are. Even if your story is true, there's the matter of at least one dead man. Folks in small towns get very peeved about having one of their own killed. We would be lynched on sight.'

At that point Harvey joined them and his partner briefly explained the situation. A couple of times their prisoner sought to interject but was quickly told to shut up. He was not a man used to taking orders but was smart enough to gauge his captors' anger.

'You want to hope that none of your men try to rescue you,' Marty told Thorpe. 'If they try, I'll shoot you on the spot.'

'I'm sure we can straighten this out. It looks like a case

of mistaken identity.'

'A mistake that cost us our pack outfit,' Harvey reminded him, 'and if you'd had your way both of us would probably be dead.'

'We could come to some agreement about your mule.'

'There's also camp gear, provisions and spare clothes,' Marty declared. 'Those buzzards of yours are over there going through our pack. We have no way of carrying away anything they leave.'

'Come back to town with me and you can make a claim for what you have lost.'

Marty was no longer inclined to argue. He prodded Thorpe with the barrel of his Winchester.

'I'm making a claim on you right now. How much money have you got on you?'

'You can't do that,' the prisoner objected. 'That's robbery.'

'Keep your hands up. Harvey, search this coyote. I reckon he owes us at least a hundred dollars.'

Harvey needed no urging and was none too gentle as he set about his task. He found a wallet in the inside pocket of Thorpe's coat. He opened it and counted the notes inside.

'Only seventy bucks here. We need another thirty at least.'

The lanky cowboy resumed searching Thorpe's other pockets but found nothing of value. Then he espied a heavy gold chain across his prisoner's vest. A tug on the chain brought a very-expensive-looking gold watch from a vest pocket. He removed the watch and chain, admired it briefly, then showed it to Marty.

'I reckon this fancy ticker would be worth thirty bucks anywhere. We'll take it and call it quits.'

'You can't take that,' Thorpe protested, his face flushed red with anger. 'That's a family heirloom. It belonged to my father. Please don't take that.'

'We were figuring to make our mule, Basil, a family heir-loom and your sonsofbitches killed him. Think yourself lucky you ain't as dead as he is.'

Thorpe was continuing to protest when Marty walked to where he had dropped one of his revolvers on the ground. He picked up the big cap-and-ball Colt and began removing the caps until only one remained.

'Here's your gun; only one chamber is capped. That grey horse of yours has a broken leg.' Marty passed the gun to Thorpe. 'Don't try anything stupid because there are two rifles on you. Go over there and shoot that poor horse – and do the job properly. Then you start walking over to where the rest of your heroes are skulking.'

'If you make one move toward that carbine on your saddle,' Harvey added, 'I'll fill you full of lead. Do you know how to shoot a horse properly? It can be tricky.'

'I've had to do it before. I'm asking you again – can't we come to some arrangement about that watch? It means a lot to me.'

'And it means thirty bucks to us,' Marty told him. 'Now shoot that horse and get going. We'll keep you covered until you reach the rest of those skunks. One more thing: we'll be watching our back trail and if we see you following we'll shoot you.'

Thorpe's face went red with anger. 'You won't get away with this. I'll hunt you down.'

It was Marty's turn to get angry. 'One more word out of you and I'll shoot you right here. Shut your mouth, shoot that horse and get walking. Otherwise you might like to try your luck against me right now with the one shot you have in that gun.'

Briefly Thorpe contemplated using his gun on his captors. In his blind rage he almost forgot there were two rifles trained on him. Then he started to think logically again and realized that further objections were likely to prove fatal. Seething with anger he walked to the grey horse, and killed it cleanly with one shot. Then he started walking towards where his men were still waiting.

Harvey kept him covered while Marty collected their horses. When Thorpe was far enough away from the rifle on the dead horse they mounted and set off at a canter.

'I have a feeling that we should have shot our friend Thorpe,' Harvey said as their two horses loped side by side.

His companion steered Lonesome around an ancient stump almost concealed in the sage before replying:

'It would only have complicated things if it turned out he was telling the truth.'

'He didn't appreciate losing that watch. It sure is a fancy one – like an award presented for something outstanding.'

'Yes,' Marty said angrily, 'like mule murdering, or stealing our outfit. It could be hard to replace some of the stuff those buzzards took.'

'Look on the bright side, partner. We can move a lot faster travelling light.'

Jason Thorpe, as he led his depleted posse back to Cedar Flats, was not as displeased as his face suggested. The plan had worked well. He had an excuse for calling off the chase and now had two likely suspects for the bank robbery. He also had a good reason to continue the hunt for them once he had escorted home the townsmen, whose indignation and enthusiasm had been dampened by the loss of a dedicated, if impulsive, citizen.

He would collect his friends Sanderson and Glasson from town where, as his deputies, they were gathering information about the bank raid. Not that he needed to know much more. He knew the men who had held up the bank and knew where to find them. The bank manager had only seen two men before he was blindfolded and did not know that three men had been involved.

16

The chance discovery of the two strangers could have been used to the gang's advantage if they had been killed. Their escape still gave Thorpe a reason to be away from town and the incident added more confusion to what had really happened.

If only they had not stolen that watch.

Thorpe had never considered losing it but was suddenly aware that such an unanticipated triviality could seriously jeopardize his meticulously laid plans for the future.

CHAPTER 3

Marty and Harvey rode hard for the rest of the day, stopping only to give their horses enough rest to keep them fit to travel. Just as the light was beginning to fade they found a patch of good grass on a small creek and staked out their horses.

An unwary antelope strayed into Marty's rifle's sights when it came to the creek to drink, so they had enough to eat, but game cooked over an open fire and eaten without salt hardly made an enjoyable meal.

'I know this beats starving,' Harvey said as he chewed on a half-burnt, half-raw rib, 'but it don't beat it by a hell of a lot.'

Marty was slicing pieces off a leg with his pocket knife. 'We'll have enough cooked meat left over for another meal or two tomorrow. I have an old newspaper in my saddle-bag. We can wrap it in that but we need to buy some proper food the first chance we get.'

Both men unrolled their slickers and spread them out for groundsheets. Then they shook out their saddle blankets and arranged the sweatiest parts as far as they could from their faces before wrapping them around themselves and settling down for a rough night's sleep.

The hours that followed were uncomfortable and morning came as a relief. Neither spoke much until they finished a breakfast of cold meat and creek water. Both were thinking longingly of their coffee pot, now in the hands of Thorpe's men.

'At least we don't have to wash our dishes and pack them up,' Marty said in an attempt to sound cheerful.

Harvey's response was to swear and fervently hope that certain 'mule-murdering skunks' would choke on the bacon and coffee they had stolen.

An uncomfortable week passed before Marty and Harvey had managed to replace most of their lost equipment at ranches and towns along the way. The further west they went the more expensive basic camping items became and the dwindling of their finances meant they had to make compromises.

Mules were not cheap but at one trading post they were able to buy a wiry little Indian pony for a couple of dollars. Another dollar bought a worn McClellan saddle, the rawhide seat covering of which was split, making it too uncomfortable for a rider. But with a bit of improvisation Marty converted it into a makeshift pack saddle. Empty corn sacks would have to serve as pack bags and a tarpaulin made a pack cover by day and a shelter at night.

Bacon was not always available but most trading posts sold jerky made from dried beef or buffalo meat. Coffee was expensive but, like salt, sugar and flour, it was deemed to be a necessity.

Extended grazing time and irregular purchases of hay and grain helped to keep their horses in good condition even though their progress had slowed considerably.

The pinto pony, which they named 'Chief', had been packed before and gave no trouble. The weather was good and once again life on the trail became a bit more comfortable, at least for those who were used to it.

No more was heard of Jason Thorpe and both men were beginning to believe that he had given up any ideas of pursuit. He had ceased to be a worry, but then eastbound travellers whom they met began to talk of Indian trouble along the trail.

Only a few years had passed since the Fetterman massacre and Red Cloud's Sioux had forced the closure of the Bozeman Trail. A shaky truce was in place but bands of hostile warriors from a variety of tribes, disregarding it, were raiding ranches and attacking coaches and wagon trains. This was the situation on the overland trail.

'There are supposed to be stagecoaches running,' Harvey observed one morning, 'but we haven't seen a sign of a coach or a wagon for a couple of days. I know we've been camping off the road where the feed is better but we're not so far away that we wouldn't see a coach if it came along.'

'I'm not too worried about coaches, Harvey, as long as our friend Thorpe doesn't show up again. I thought he would be after us even if only to get his watch back.'

'That watch might not mean much to Thorpe at all. The engraving on the back says: *To Major Thomas Sutcliffe, Kansas Volunteers, 1859.*'

'Didn't Thorpe say that was his father's watch?' Marty asked. 'Do you think he was lying to us about it being a family heirloom?'

'Probably. Some of these small-town lawmen are so dang crooked that they have to screw their socks on. I reckon he took it off someone else. But there's something funny about that date. It's too late for the Mexican War and too early for the Civil War.'

'It has to be the Kansas-Missouri border wars. We were only kids at the time but I remember that we heard about them way down in Texas. Our main worry was Comanches and Kiowas, but if stories were true they were gentlemen compared to the Kansas abolitionists and the Missouri bushwhackers. They were so bad that both sides finished up disowning them in the Civil War. By all accounts the law's still looking for a lot of Bill Quantrill's men.'

'Could be that Thorpe's old man was on the Kansas side and that he, or his son, changed his name later. Then there's the chance that he was on the other side and took the watch from one of their victims. Either way, I don't give a rat's rear end.'

When they rode on to the main trail there was no mistaking it. Thousands of hoofs and wheels had cut a track nearly a hundred yards wide, and in places the iron tyres of heavily laden wagons had worn grooves several inches deep in some of the rocks. Any vegetation that had once grown there had now been trampled into dust, leaving a long, dusty scar that pointed to the West.

From long habit the two travellers read the tracks on the ground and were surprised that all led in the same direction.

'We must be headed for a real good place,' Harvey said, 'because there's no recent trace of anyone coming the other way.'

The grey sagebrush-covered plains were gradually giving way to hill country, much of it clothed in dark-green vegetation. They crossed a succession of north-south ridges and saw, from one high point, the crests of the Rocky Mountains as a hazy purple line in the far distance. But before they reached that point the riders had seen rising smoke.

'It ain't a signal,' 'Harvey said. 'Must be a big camp of some kind.'

Marty watched the smoke for a while.

'It would be white men, I reckon,' he told his partner. 'Indians don't advertise their presence like that in daytime.'

Half an hour later the riders crossed a low ridge. In the shallow valley beyond it they saw hundreds of animals grazing. There were horses, mules and oxen spread over the entire grassy area. Some animals were hobbled and several were fitted with bells. Around the area were mounted guards, most of whom seemed to be carrying rifles. Some patrolled the fringes of the herd, turning back animals that attempted to move out of the area. Other guards had dismounted and were holding their horses in the shade of a cottonwood grove as they talked and smoked in small groups.

A tree-lined creek ran down the western side of the hollow; beyond that were clusters of tents and parked vehicles, mostly wagons of various sizes but a couple of stagecoaches could also be seen. The newcomers could discern the distant figures of people moving among the great variety of temporary shelters.

'What's going on here?' Harvey asked as he surveyed the strange scene.

'Ain't nothing I've ever seen,' Marty replied. 'Looks like a regular town is being set up. There's a fella over there to our left on a buckskin horse. Let's ask him.'

They rode across to the guard, a shaggy-haired youth armed with a long, muzzle-loading squirrel rifle. The briefest of introductions was followed by a string of questions which the guard answered in a slow Southern drawl.

'It's Injun trouble,' he explained. 'They closed about sixty miles of trail and cut the telegraph wires. Stories are that they burned a couple of stage stations and wiped out a ranch or two as well. The army's closed a big stretch of trail – won't let through any bunch of travellers that has less than a hundred armed men.'

'What else are the army doing about this?' Marty asked.

'I don't rightly know. Best you ask Captain Farrell. We've been told to direct anyone who comes along to report to him. He has a tent just near the crick crossin'. You'll see a couple of them brass-button soldiers outside it.'

'Much obliged,' Marty said. He turned Lonesome towards the chaotic scene ahead.

*

Jason Thorpe was not a happy man. His carefully laid plans were unravelling. It would have been so convenient to pin the blame for the bank robbery on the two passing strangers, and then kill them before they could protest their innocence. A story that the bandits had somehow hidden their loot would have generated a horde of gullible hopefuls whose inquiries and searches would have only added to the confusion.

But Marty and Harvey had not cooperated and, by their survival, had seriously jeopardized the future that he had so carefully mapped out.

Years before some of his partisan associates had warned about keeping that gold watch but he retained it, arguing that it contributed to his image as a prosperous, respectable citizen. After all, what stranger would he allow to read the inscription on the back of the case? The watch and its recovery, however, had suddenly became a minor distraction in the present circumstances.

The Cedar Flat bank robbery had gone without a hitch. Lane, Cooper and Kirk had grabbed the bank manager, Saunders, before opening time and had cleaned out the bank before the rest of the townspeople became aware of what was occurring. The loot was thrown hastily into a couple of wheat sacks: notes and coins of various denominations mixed in together.

The much-disturbed bank manager could not put an accurate figure on the amount stolen because the bank's books were not as up to date as they should have been. He could only say that 'several thousand dollars' had been taken.

As town marshal Thorpe had acted quickly when the theft was discovered; first by raising a posse of sorts, then deliberately leading them the wrong way. According to the plan, the three robbers were to head for a secure hideout east of Omaha with the loot. A coded letter to Thorpe, care of the marshal's office, would confirm when the bandits were safely hidden. After a suitable period of fruitless searching Thorpe and his two deputies would resign their jobs and join the rest of the gang to collect their share of the takings.

That was the plan. Then things went awry.

The brush with Marty and Harvey had caused a few problems but, on the positive side, it helped to convince the people at Cedar Flat that their marshal had been on the right trail.

The coded telegram from Nebraska was late in coming but the sender confirmed that the trio had not arrived at the hideout, nor had they been seen in the vicinity. Thorpe knew then that he had been double-crossed.

He called upon John Sanderson and Ed Glasson, his part-time deputies in Cedar Flat, who had also been full-time associates during earlier guerilla activities. Any virtues this pair might have possessed were well hidden but they had proved themselves loyal to Thorpe and were probably the only people he really trusted.

All three were survivors of Quantrill's guerillas who had evaded capture at the Civil War's end and who had quietly resumed peaceful lives under assumed names.

Sanderson was a gaunt, hollow-cheeked man in his early forties. In his partisan days he had been conspicuous because of his wild, shoulder-length hair and thick black beard. Now he was clean-shaven, quietly spoken and neatly dressed, the epitome of respectability. He made no great show of armaments, wearing a Colt .38 high on his right hip, but carrying a shortened version of the same revolver in an inside pocket of the leather vest that he wore. A sharp-pointed Arkansas Toothpick in a rawhide sheath was also concealed in his right boot. Over the last twelve years he had slain so many people that he had become desensitized and would kill without a second thought.

Glasson, who was a few years younger, had joined Quantrill midway through the latter's bloody career. Of average size, with a youthful face, he looked innocent enough but his cold, pale-blue eyes and the solid muscle that filled out his neat town clothes were the signs of a dangerous man. Several men had missed or ignored the subtle warnings and had paid for it with their lives. In his guerilla days he had been an admirer of Arch Clements, a pint-sized killer who had made Bloody Bill Anderson look like a choirboy. Glasson had kept up with modern technology and sported a pair of the latest Smith & Wesson .44s. He made no effort to be sociable and, in his role as Thorpe's deputy, he had caused considerable unease among the citizens of Cedar Flat. Under instructions not to alienate the townspeople he reluctantly refrained from gunplay but he would use his fists very effectively if his authority was challenged.

Lane, Cooper and Kirk had been hiding in various places since the end of the Civil War. In true guerilla style they would come together under Thorpe's leadership to rob a coach or a bank or a prosperous businessman. More than once they had left corpses behind them but then they would quickly disperse into remote, secure hideouts. The law could never find them but their old comrades knew how to reach them. It was their ability to lose pursuers that led Thorpe to use them for the actual robbery. He had never expected the trio to betray him.

'I should have known better than to trust those reptiles,' he complained to Sanderson, 'but they ain't as smart as they think. They laid a false trail, thinking it would be weeks before we found out we'd been robbed. I didn't tell them that I had a few spies watching for them.'

Sanderson agreed that their associates had been less

than honest with them and that they needed to be hunted down before they could split up and spend the loot.

'We need to catch 'em quick,' he said. 'But where do we start looking? The West's a mighty big place.'

'It is, but roads are few. We know they haven't gone east. My guess is that they have taken the overland trail. It has cut-offs that can take them to California or Oregon or Santa Fe and a heap of people still use it.'

Sanderson remained unconvinced.

'Even if they headed the way you think, they'd be a long way ahead. Chances are that they've already split the money and gone their separate ways.'

'That may be, but I reckon that as soon as they think they're safely away, they'll start spending money in a big way in towns along the trail and they will move slowly. We all know how serious hangovers discourage early morning starts. And there are newspaper reports of traffic along the trail being stopped. There's big trouble with Indians and they've cut the transcontinental telegraph line in several places. It's said they've been attacking travellers, freighters and ranch people.'

'How does that affect us?'

'The army is stopping traffic on both sides of the damaged section. They won't let people go through unless they are in a group with at least a hundred armed men. Even then a lot of folks ain't prepared to take the chance. They are waiting at the road barriers until everything is declared safe again. Those thieving coyotes might not be as far away as we thought. I'm going after them. Are you and Glasson with me?'

'Count me in,' Sanderson replied, 'and I reckon Glasson will go along with us when we tell him. It will take a day or two though, to get our pack outfit together.'

'We leave tomorrow morning. Don't worry about packs. There will be towns, trading posts and ranches and homesteads where we can buy food. We can sleep in hotels or barns, whatever we find. If our horses start to fail we sell them and buy others. We travel light and fast, just like the old days.'

'Not quite like the old days,' Sanderson corrected. 'We didn't pay for replacement horses then.'

CHAPTER 4

Captain Bartholemew Farrell of the 22nd Infantry was a very stressed man. For more than a week he had been camped near the creek crossing, checking new arrivals and answering the same questions and complaints.

The main query was why cavalry escorts could not be provided for west-bound travellers. The fact that the nation's east-west communications were severed mattered little to the ever-growing and increasingly impatient crowd gathered at the barrier.

Marty and Harvey were the latest arrivals to try the captain's patience, but in them he saw what could be a partial solution to his problem. The first group prepared to travel without an escort had almost reached the required number of one hundred armed men. He would check the list he was compiling and as soon as the quota of armed men was met he would be able to reduce the size of the camp.

'Why aren't there any cavalry for escort work?' Marty asked.

'Because there are only two companies to cover a couple of hundred miles of trail. Our Indian friends have cut the telegraph line in several places. The country's most important communications have been cut in half and the government has made fixing them the first priority.'

'But surely it wouldn't take long to join the wires again?'

Harvey queried.

'The wires are not the problem. It's the poles. The Indians are a bit wary of taking the wires these days. Our scouts have brought back stories of hostiles who were dragging away about a hundred feet of stolen wire when a thunderstorm came. Lightning struck the wire that was being dragged behind their ponies. Stories vary about how many warriors were killed but they are reluctant to take wire now.'

'So what's the problem with the poles?' Marty asked.

In a bored voice Farrell repeated the answer he had given on numerous occasions:

'I was about to say that telegraph poles don't grow on trees, but we all know they do. There are no useful trees in the area where the poles were destroyed. The nearest suitable trees are in a canyon nearly fifty miles from here. Wagons have to be escorted to get the poles and then deliver them safely to where the cavalry are also planting them again. The men replacing the poles have to be guarded, as do the empty wagons going back for more poles.

'Those poor devils are working around the clock and they have to be rotated from pole-cutting, to pole-planting, to wire-stringing and escort duty. To add insult to injury, the Indians used the original poles to cook big numbers of cattle stolen from local ranches.'

'So what do we do now?' Marty asked.

'If you are prepared to become part of an armed group of at least a hundred men, give your names to a wagon boss named Gus Ransom. You'll see his big Conestoga wagon over there under the trees. When he gets the required number of men I will allow him to go. I think your extra guns would be welcome.'

Oscar Lane, Jim Cooper and Albert Kirk had covered their

tracks well. In dirty, worn work clothes, with unkempt beards and battered hats, they looked nothing like the trio who had robbed the bank at Cedar Flat. Their fine horses had been replaced by six sturdy mules and a light wagon. They looked like another group of poor sodbusters who had pooled their resources to seek their fortunes farther west.

Each wore a converted Colt rimfire .44 on the hip. And, for appearances' sake, Lane and Cooper had a couple of army-surplus muzzle-loading rifles while Kirk had a double-barreled shotgun. Three modern Winchester repeaters were concealed in the wagon under some saddles and bedding. Also hidden, among grain sacks for the mules, were the two bundles of stolen cash, still in crumpled sacks.

In case faster movement became necessary, the team mules had been broken to saddle and pack as well as harness. They would suffice until faster horses could be obtained. The wagon could be abandoned if their pursuers were found to be getting close.

Gus Ransom, when Marty and Harvey found him, turned out to be a small, bald man who had been a major in the Confederate army during the Civil War. He carried his left arm awkwardly as the result of an old wound but had spent most of his life on the frontier and had a reputation as an Indian-fighter.

He was pleased to accept the newcomers as part of his group, especially when he found that they had fought Indians before. Although many of his party had guns, some had never fired a shot in anger.

The bank robbers fitted easily into the restless assembly, among which just about every frontier occupation was represented. There were townsmen going West to start new businesses, the Gilbert sisters who hoped to open a dress-making and clothing establishment, a lawyer, a couple of surveyors, various tradesmen, freighters and many would-be ranchers and homesteaders. Additionally there were buffalo hunters, gunmen, gamblers, prospectors, opportunists of all kinds, and more than one army deserter. There were drifters and men who said little about themselves. Many were former soldiers from the Civil War.

Three stagecoaches were also stranded and not all their passengers were eager to take their chances on what could be a very dangerous journey. By way of compromise it was agreed that the reluctant travellers would remain at the road block until safety was assured but two coaches would be included in Ransom's group.

The Gilbert sisters would be the only women in the party. Young and unattached, they were seeking a new start in territory far away from the Civil War's scarred battlefields and areas where old hatreds still lingered. Their father had been killed in the war and their mother died shortly after it ended. Taken in grudgingly by relatives, the two orphans were trained as seamstresses and their talents exploited until both felt old enough and skilled enough to strike out on their own. They pooled their meagre savings, bought a sewing machine and headed West with hope in their hearts and a determination to succeed. Judy was the elder. At twenty-two she was mature beyond her years, an attractive lady with a trim figure and dark curly hair. She was the planner of the pair, quiet by nature but never aloof. During their adolescent years she had taken responsibility for her younger sister and protected her in an environment in which the two had been barely tolerated until they could be put to work.

Marjie was twenty, with blonde hair, a pretty face and a smile that came readily when she was pleased. Judy had shielded her sister from some of the battles that would ultimately shape their personalities, so the younger woman's outlook on life was much more relaxed. Her happy, trusting nature was a worry to her sister, considering the rough company in which they found themselves. Marjie had proved that she was capable of looking after herself but her sister was still very protective of her.

Both looked a treat in their stylish, home-made dresses and Ransom had no problem getting volunteers to guard the coach.

'That wagon is one of mine,' the wagon boss told the two Texans as he pointed to one standing near by. 'The driver's name is Joe Grimmett. You can throw your pack in there and hitch your pony to the tailboard, or let it be driven loose with the spare stock, whatever you want.'

'I reckon we'll hitch it to the back of Grimmett's wagon,' Harvey told him. 'If the Indians do hit us, they'll try to drive away any loose stock.'

'We've been a mite unlucky with our pack animals of late, so we don't want to risk losing this one,' Marty explained.

'Where will we be best when the outfit is rolling?' Harvey asked.

'You boys would be mighty helpful if you rode wide on the left of the train and kept a sharp lookout. We don't want any nasty surprises. Keep out as far as is safe but keep the wagons in sight and keep an eye on each other. Indians are pretty good at cutting off individual riders. I'll be in front with a couple of scouts out ahead of me and there'll be more guards out on the right side. There will be others escorting the teamsters in close to the wagons and a few more acting as a rearguard. If you strike trouble come back to the wagons in case you get shot by our own men. Some of these characters are unknown quantities in a fight. Too many are volunteering to guard the coach with the two Gilbert girls instead of being around the edges of the train where they could do the most good. But maybe it's better that they don't get under foot if trouble starts. Now, get yourselves organized because Farrell says we have enough men to start in the morning.'

*

Thorpe and his men arrived just as night was falling. Like all newcomers they registered with Farrell and announced their intention to go with Ransom's train.

As Thorpe had predicted, they had been able to buy meals, a supply of jerky and whiskey to sustain them on nights when they camped away from other habitations. The supply problem for the next day or two was solved when they found that a couple of enterprising characters named Saville and James had loaded two wagons with bacon, beans, flour, salt, sugar, coffee and an array of cooking utensils. They would prepare and sell the basics needed by their fellow travellers for meals over the expected three-day journey. They had even agreed to buy any game brought in by Ambrose Costa, an old mountain man who had joined the train.

The camp seethed with activity as those who had elected to continue their journeys were checking with Ransom to determine where they should travel, or were assembling their belongings for an early-morning start.

There were debts to settle as a few gamblers had found rich pickings among the stranded travellers. A considerable amount of last-minute trading was also taking place.

'Seems to me,' Harvey told his friend, 'that this might be a good time to cash in that watch. This camp is a regular trading post and quite a few of these pilgrims are well-heeled.'

'It's worth a try. If you have any luck, there's a farmer up the hill there selling corn. For another ten cents he'll put it through a cracker he has attached to the tailboard of his wagon. A sack of that would be very handy for our horses in case the wagons have to circle somewhere. I don't know if Chief knows what corn is but we'll have to give him a little bit at a time. Now's as good a time as any to get him started.'

'Aren't you coming with me?' the tall cowboy asked.

'I'll join you later. I want to trim some of that split rawhide off our pack saddle. It's dried hard and could make a sharp edge under the tree. I thought I'd fix it while we have time.'

Harvey laughed. 'I was thinking we might go later and win the hearts of them two pretty girls at the coach.'

'We wouldn't get near them. There must be half a dozen hopefuls surrounding them and they would not be attracted to a couple of rough-looking critters like us.'

Mortimer Jennings was a little man with a hard face and an even harder heart. He would deal in any commodity likely to return him a profit on the transaction. If his fellow men expected a fair deal from him they were rapidly disillusioned.

His latest prospective customer looked like an easy victim and the gold watch that Harvey showed him certainly caught his attention. Even in the dim lantern light from a nearby wagon he could see that it was a quality piece, but he adopted a seemingly casual, almost uninterested, attitude.

'What do you want for it?' he said out of the corner of his mouth.

Harvey thought he would aim high. 'How about forty bucks?'

Jennings frowned, then snapped, 'Ten bucks is my top offer. For all I know that thing could be stolen. Where did you get it?'

'It was used to settle a debt but my partner and I would prefer to turn it into cash.'

Jennings opened the back with an air of disdain, held the watch closer to the lantern and read the inscription.

'Did you get this from its owner?'

'No. I reckon there might have been a couple of owners since it was presented to Major Sutcliffe. The fella who

34

traded it reckoned it was a family heirloom so he must have inherited it.'

'You ain't from Kansas, are you?'

'Not till we delivered a herd of Texas cattle a couple of weeks ago. What's Kansas got to do with this?'

'Sonny,' Jennings passed the watch back to Harvey, 'that watch could get someone killed. It is connected to one of the most notorious killings of the Border wars. I used to live in Kansas at a place called Lawrence. So did Major Sutcliffe, this fancy ticker's original owner. He raised a force of abolitionist militia and for a while they played hell with the Missouri bushwhackers. He was given that watch in recognition for his services. I never knew him personally but most folks in Lawrence know what happened him.'

'I ain't from Lawrence, so let me know just why this watch is so dangerous.'

'One morning in 1863,' Jennings continued, 'Quantrill's guerillas surrounded the town and started settling a few old scores. Folks woke up to gunfire and burning houses.

'Qantrill's men rounded up everyone as they ran on to the streets, shooting anyone they disliked or who tried to escape them. They started looting the town and setting buildings alight.They also had a list of their enemies – and most of those they shot on sight.

'I was in the middle of a bunch of prisoners and saw a lot of what happened. They found Sutcliffe in a house just near us and one guerilla dragged him in to the street. A big, ugly son of a bitch with a broken nose had him by the shirt front and was about to blow his brains out when he saw his victim's watch and chain. I didn't hear what was said but people who were closer said that the guerilla took the watch and said he was worried it might get broken. Sutcliffe was still cussing him when he got a bullet through his head.

'The killer left him lying in the street while he admired the watch and then he put it in his pocket and strolled away to set fire to a nearby hotel. That was the only time I saw that watch until you turned up with it tonight. The question in my mind is, how did you get it?'

'I ain't saying just yet. Did Sutcliffe's murderer have a name?'

'He must have had one but I never heard what it was. After the war I heard that the law was looking for members of Quantrill's outfit but I never heard of anyone being arrested for the Sutcliffe killing. So far as I know the murderer is still on the loose and that watch will tie him to the crime. I doubt he'd be so dumb as to try to sell it.'

'Maybe he's dead and a relative inherited the watch,' Harvey suggested hopefully.

'Nobody who knows the history of that watch would admit to having it. Most likely it was stolen by Sutcliffe's killer – and if that low-down critter is still alive he would be rather keen to get it back. I won't even ask you how you got that fancy timepiece but my advice to you would be to throw it in a river somewhere and keep well away from any big guy you see aged about fifty with a badly busted nose.'

As he returned the watch to his pocket Harvey thought immediately of how well Jennings had described Jason Thorpe.

Lane brought the news that his companions least wanted to hear.

'I just saw Thorpe,' he said urgently. 'He was talking to that army officer. There were two other riders with him. I couldn't see them plainly in the bad light but you can bet they will be Glasson and Sanderson.'

Cooper had been filling his pipe while seated on a rock near their small campfire. He jumped to his feet.

'Did he see you?' he asked.

'I ain't that stupid,' Lane declared. Then he added, 'I ain't the one that suggested we all stay together instead of splitting the loot and taking separate trails.'

Cooper snorted like an angry bull. 'You know damn well that this money's all mixed in together. We won't even know how much we have until we can get somewhere on our own to count it and split it evenly.'

Kirk, who had been sorting out the mule harness for the morning, also snarled back.

'It might not have been the smartest plan but no sonofabitch has come up with a better one. Thorpe would expect us to use the old guerilla trick and disperse. He'll be looking for single riders whooping it up in saloons, men with good horses and more money than they should have. He won't notice three poor sodbusters creeping along in a wagon. Don't panic. This is a big train and we should only be together for three days.'

'That's three days too long,' Cooper growled. 'You can bet Thorpe will be giving this train plenty of attention. Somehow we need to keep right out of his way without drawing attention to ourselves.'

Suddenly Kirk snapped his fingers. 'I got it! I know how to shake them hounds off our trail.'

'You'd better be right this time,' Cooper said ominously.

'What's a real nasty disease that has killed people by the dozen on the way West?'

'Lead poisoning?' Lane suggested. He was wary of some of Kirk's bright ideas.

'Very smart. What about cholera?'

'Don't play games. I'm not in the mood for it,' Cooper told him. 'Any good ideas will be welcome as of now but they need to be *good* ones,'

'Just settle down and listen. Suppose we start off with the train tomorrow with two of us keeping out of sight in the wagon. We go a couple of miles with the others and then pull out. When someone asks what the trouble is, the driver says that he suspects his two partners have cholera. He says he will camp well away from the train until he knows what the trouble is. Cholera is reckoned to be very contagious and nobody with any brains goes near a cholera case. Thorpe won't want to hang around any place where that disease is suspected. Once he's ahead of us we can turn back after a day or two – or even leave the wagon, share out the loot and get away on the mules.'

'It might work,' Lane conceded grudgingly.

'It has to work,' Cooper asserted. 'If Thorpe catches up with us someone is gonna get killed.'

Marty found Harvey watching a poker game being played with the cards on a blanket beside a large fire.

Ambrose Costa was winning and the three losers, who had considered themselves skilled players, were far from happy. The old mountain man's derisive remarks irritated them greatly and they were beginning to suspect that his losses in previous games were due to cunning rather than ineptitude or bad luck. As he shuffled the cards Costa was chuckling.

'Hurry up and lose your money, gents,' he said. 'I have to make an early start in the morning. I want to get a deer to sell to them cooks before the wagons scare 'em away.'

'I hope you haven't gambled away what you got for that watch,' Marty joked as he ranged himself beside his partner.

'I was waiting for you to come by. I have some bad news about the watch. Let's go somewhere quiet and I'll tell you a sad story,' Harvey whispered.

CHAPTER 5

The camp was already astir when the first red streaks of dawn appeared on the eastern horizon. Teams and riding stock had been brought in and picketed close to their owners. Vehicles were packed, with only a few necessary items of camp gear remaining to be thrown aboard when breakfast was finished.

Judy and Marjie had not slept well in the coach but it was more comfortable and private than the hard ground where the five male passengers, the driver and the guard had been forced to sleep.

The enterprising Saville and James had supplied a breakfast of bacon, beans, thick slices of sourdough bread and black unsweetened coffee. Each traveller also added an extra nickel to the bill to cover the cost of washing the used dishes. The second shift for breakfast would be those who had chosen not to go with the wagon train and had not brought their own supplies. These would be served before the first group left camp but after that they would need to make other dining arrangements.

'It will be nice to be moving again,' Marjie said, 'even if the coach is slowed to the same pace as the wagons.'

'That's because they can't change the horses,' Judy explained. 'The Indians are said to have wiped out the stage stations along a big stretch of road. Captain Farrell told me so yesterday.'

'So you have another secret admirer. The captain will be sorry to see you go.'

'I assure you, I have no intention of marrying a soldier and being shuffled around desolate military posts for years. I want to find a nice town and set up our business before I would even consider marriage. Even then I would want a husband with a stable lifestyle. There are too many drifters here on the frontier.'

'Don't worry, sis. I'm sure that big fellow over there with the red beard and the smitten expression on his face would have a stable lifestyle because it looks as though he's spent plenty of time in stables. He'll be one of our guards today. With a shave, a bath, some new clothes and a slight improvement in manners he might be quite a good catch for you.'

'That's enough about romance. We'd best get our luggage to Mr Thomas so that he can pack it properly on the coach. We need to be ready when we see Mr Ransom's wagon move off.'

Just then Thorpe and his two companions rode out from behind a line of wagons. They were looking about, grim-faced, as they guided their horses around people and conveyances.

Thorpe saw the two sisters and tipped his hat to them but there was no warmth or respect in the gesture. It was simply a part of the role he played when he was pretending to be respectable. He did not know that the men he sought were already aware of his presence and that they had been dodging him around wagons and using various subterfuges to conceal their faces.

'That man looked very serious. He has a face like the knocker on the morgue door,' Marjie said when the riders were out of earshot. 'It's as though he was looking for someone.'

'He has the look of a lawman,' Judy replied. 'He's probably making sure there are no criminals travelling with us.'

Marty and Harvey had commenced their work early. Along with Ambrose and another frontiersman they had been sent out by Ransom to scout the trail ahead. They were out of the camp long before Thorpe and his men had started their search.

Their inability to sell the watch did not worry them greatly. Jennings was notoriously mean. According to Ambrose, he was a double-dealing little skunk who would not give a person a fright if he was a ghost. Marty suspected that the dealer might have concocted the story and might offer them a rock-bottom price later, but Harvey was inclined to believe the tale.

'A few people told me that Jennings was a slippery little skunk,' he said, 'but to me he looked really scared. Maybe for once in his life he told the truth.'

There had been a considerable amount of traffic in the proximity of the camp and for the first hour the scouts could find no evidence of Indian presence among so many tracks. The terrain was almost flat and in a few places they saw small clumps of scrubby trees but nowhere that would conceal a large war party.

Eventually they reached a small creek where they saw the charred remains of a building and what had once been a sizeable corral. Several large patches of burnt ground showed where cattle had been killed and cooked on fires made from corral poles. The area was littered with cattle bones, cast aside first by the Indians and then spread further by coyotes, wolves and other scavengers.

Harvey was the closest; he called for Marty to join him, then he saw Ambrose and his partner approaching from the other side. The old man had a pronghorn antelope tied behind his saddle.

'See anything?' the mountain man asked.

'Not until now and none of this sign seems to be fresh. Marty might have seen something. He'll be here in a minute. What about you?'

Ambrose bit off a piece of chewing tobacco, tucking it inside his cheek before replying:

'There's a broad trail headin' north but it's an old one. I reckon them varmints just kept goin' after they filled up on stolen beef. The antelope would have moved away if the Injuns were hangin' about.'

'That won't go far among more than a hundred people.' Harvey pointed to the dead antelope.

'Who cares? Them grub spoilers are payin' me two dollars a head for anything I bring in, cleaned and dressed. With any luck I'll pick up another one around sundown. Four dollars a day is good money.'

'Beats driving cows,' Harvey admitted.

Marty joined them. He had picked up the war party's trail as the raiders came from the south but had found no signs of recent activity. He indicated the black patches where the fires had been.

'I hope it was only cattle being cooked there.'

'I heard that the change station crew had some sort of warning and got out,' Ambrose replied, 'but we have to pass two more of these stations and the poor souls there might not have been so lucky.'

The mountain man's partner, a taciturn half-breed, suddenly pointed back along the trail to where a large dust cloud was rising. Ransom and the main party were on their way.

'It's about time,' Harvey said.

'Somethin' must've delayed 'em,' the scout speculated. 'Ain't like Ransom to be runnin' late.'

'How far are we from tonight's camp site?' Marty asked.

'It's about ten miles,' Ambrose replied. 'It was a change

station for the coaches on Carolina Creek, but I doubt there'll be much left of it. I heard that an army patrol found and buried what was left of the four coach company men that the Indians killed when they came through. The creek has the best water we'll find on this trip and the grass is usually good, so the teams can get a good bellyful. We'll scout a couple of miles beyond the camp just in case some of them hostiles have doubled back. It's a good place for them to rest up.'

All agreed that it was best not to get too far ahead of Ransom's train in case a war party would slip in behind them. They watered their horses at the creek before dismounting in the thin shade of a few willows that grew on the bank.

Nearly an hour later the advance guard of the wagons arrived. Ransom was not with them.

'You took your time, 'Ambrose complained. 'At this rate the wagons will be making camp in the dark at Carolina Creek.'

The foremost newcomer was nearly as old as the mountain man and his lined face seemed to be set in a permanent scowl that had earned him the ironic name of Happy.

'There's been trouble. Looks like cholera. Three sodbusters travelling together have reported cholera. Two of 'em are laid up and the one driving their wagon could catch it too. Ransom couldn't leave them at the road camp and the best idea was to cut out the wagon and let it tail along behind. There's no doctors to be had and those three will have to take their chances on their own. Ransom is going to set up a camp for them here, and they'll move into it after the train leaves.'

'But three sick men can't look after each other,' Marty said.

'It appears that the fit one has had cholera once before

and some people claim it makes him proof against the disease.'

'I ain't sure that's right.' Ambrose sounded doubtful, 'But I do know it's best to keep right away from cholera cases.'

'They could starve to death if they all catch it,' Harvey reminded. Happy nodded in agreement but told them:

'Them two Gilbert gals thought of that. They've been goin' around collectin' food that will keep for a few days. It was left close to the wagon. The fit fella's name is Brown and he was seen to pick it up and take it to the wagon. Ransom said he'll send someone back tomorrow to check on how things are.'

'We could meet folks comin' the other way now that the trail's open,' Ambrose suggested. 'I think we should warn them about approachin' a lone wagon. We don't want them pickin' up the disease and takin' it back East again.'

'Time we got moving,' Marty said as he watched the leading wagons appear from around a low hill. 'If this Carolina Creek is such a good place to camp, Indians could still be hanging about there.'

Thorpe was watering his horse at the first break in his journey when the little stranger dismounted from his heavily laden mule and led it to the water. The big man paid him scant notice because his mind was on the search for his former associates. But the newcomer rapidly gained his attention when he said, out of the corner of his mouth:

'You look like a man who's lost a watch.'

Thorpe was shocked. He was sure that he had never met this man who seemed to know about the watch that had been taken from him. His big worry was that the man probably knew his identity and how he had acquired Sutcliffe's presentation timepiece.

'Do I know you?' he demanded.

'We ain't never met,' Jennings replied but did not elaborate further.

'What makes you think that I'd be interested in buying a cheap watch from a stranger like you?'

'I ain't selling a watch, but for twenty dollars I'll tell you who is the person in this group who tried to sell me a watch presented to a certain Major Sutcliffe.'

'I don't know any Sutcliffe and I sure as hell don't intend paying any money for a story about a stolen watch. You're barking up the wrong tree, my friend.'

Shrugging his shoulders Jennings pretended to believe the big man.

'I must have you mixed up with someone else, but for what it's worth, the young fella concerned said last night that the watch was not stolen and he took it to square a debt.'

It was the latter statement that told Thorpe what he needed to know: that the watch was still with the man who had taken it from him and that he was travelling with the wagon train. However, his carefully concealed excitement was diminished slightly by the fact that Jennings knew his identity. The little man would betray him if he knew of the reward offered years before for his capture or death.

The risk was too great. Jennings would have to be silenced.

Darkness had fallen by the time the collection of travellers reached Carolina Creek, where another problem presented itself.

As a camping site the location had been heavily used in recent times by raiding Indians and army patrols. The water was good and plentiful, the grazing was sparse but would do for an overnight stop. The main problem was the lack of firewood.

Ransom directed the setting up of the camp and then

ordered men out in all directions to collect wood. Without it there would not be enough fuel for cooking the evening meals and next morning's breakfast. Although guards were still placed around the camp's perimeter, the wagon boss had been assured by the outriders that there were no recent signs of hostile warriors.

Seeking fuel, some small groups went out with lanterns but other wood collectors searched relying solely upon their night vision. Some carried the sticks back in sacks but others just carried them in their arms. When a man had a full load he returned and dumped the wood on a central pile which was steadily growing. But it would need to grow much more as the available fuel was only lightweight and would burn quickly.

Jennings had no intention of collecting wood but moved out of camp anyway so that he would not appear to be loafing amid such activity. He took no light, trusting to his night vision as he made his way to a low hill that would afford him a good view of the camp. He thought he was alone but he was wrong.

Sanderson, on Thorpe's instructions, had been discreetly watching the trader all day. The man had to be silenced lest he should let slip some information that could lead to the fake lawman's real identity being revealed.

Jennings had seated himself on a rock but there was no cover near by that afforded the former guerilla a concealed approach to his victim. In the dim light a shot was likely to miss and would alert people in the camp. The only sure way to get his man would be to use his knife and take his victim by surprise.

Abandoning all stealth, Sanderson slipped the knife from the sheath in his boot but kept it close to his body where it would not be seen. Then he noisily forced his way through a few low-growing bushes.

'Hey pardner,' he called softly. 'Have you found any

useful firewood around here?'

'Not a single stick,' came the reply.

'Looks like we both climbed this damned hill for nothing,' Sanderson muttered as he closed the distance between them.

'Seems we did,' Jennings agreed. He was not interested in making small talk. His thoughts were concentrated upon how best to deal with a dangerous man like Thorpe.

Sanderson gestured towards the fire that was glowing plainly in the centre of the camp.

'What the hell are they doin' down there?'

Instinctively the little man looked in the direction indicated. A powerful hand was clamped across his mouth and a long sharp blade was driven up under his ribs. A muffled grunt was the only sound Jennings made as he went rigid and then fell limply as his killer let him drop.

Sanderson withdrew his knife, wiped it clean on his victim's coat and then, after checking to be sure he had avoided bloodstains on his own person, he proceeded to ransack Jennings' pockets. Like many professionals who killed unsuspecting victims with knives, he knew how to avoid the rush of blood that followed the stab. Working carefully, he found a small Colt .22 revolver, a thick roll of notes and a few dollars in loose change. He transferred these to his own pockets, then proceeded to scalp his victim.

CHAPTER 6

Daylight was just starting to creep across the landscape when an alert guard on the camp perimeter sighted something on a little hill about a hundred and fifty yards away. At first it looked like a bundle of old clothes but then, as the light improved, the guard's curiosity turned to alarm.

'Injuns,' he screamed. 'It's Injuns!'

The camp came alive as the early-risers ceased their tasks, grabbed their weapons and hurried to join the crowd that was gathering around the shocked sentry.

'Over there on the hill,' he gasped. 'That's a dead man. He's sorta crumpled up but he ain't moved since I saw him just on daylight. He's dead for sure.'

A collective gasp was followed by confused speculation as various individuals reacted to the situation. Suddenly all were prepared to believe the dire warnings they had been given about hostile Indians.

Ransom emerged from his wagon, buckling his gun belt as he came. Angrily he brushed his way through the rapidly assembling mob and bellowed at them.

'Get to your posts, you jackasses. Do you want to lose all the livestock? This might only be a diversion to keep us looking the other way.'

A few saw his logic and obeyed the wagon boss; but others, more curious than cautious, remained where they were, clustering around Ransom asking questions and offering opinions.

It was Thorpe who brought some order to the situation. He steered his horse through the onlookers with Sanderson and Glasson riding closely behind him. He checked his mount beside the wagon master and leaned down before speaking quietly.

'If you can organize things here, my deputies and I will go up to that hill and see if there are any Indians hanging about. Have a couple of good shots with repeating rifles ready to cover us from here. We might need to come back in a hurry.'

'I'm mighty obliged,' Ransom responded. 'I was about to call for volunteers. Don't take any chances out there. That dead man might have been left as bait to lure a few of us out.'

Thorpe made no reply but drew his Spencer repeater from its saddle scabbard and held it across the pommel ready for action. His two followers did likewise with their carbines as they urged their horses away from the camp.

They rode together until they were out of earshot of the others. Then Thorpe spoke quietly.

'Spread out and go each side of that hill. I'll go straight at it. Once you're out of sight of the wagons, make a lot of tracks to blot out any signs of what happened last night. Some of those old mountain men are good trackers. I'll do the same here and anyone watching will think I'm looking for Indian sign. When you see me on the hilltop, join me there and we'll go and have a look at Jennings' remains. By the way, John,' he turned to Sanderson, 'you're getting sloppy. I can see blood on your left boot. When you get out of sight, check that you haven't picked up any more stains.'

'Don't worry, Jason. I'll scuff my boot in a bit of loose dirt. That'll stick to it and cover it up. Those nervous Nellies back in the camp will be too busy looking for Indians to be looking at my boots.'

Marty and Harvey were saddling their horses and did not join the spectators who were watching Thorpe and his men. But they were close enough to see that the man they most wanted to avoid had joined the train.

Harvey was first to recognize the big man, although he did not know his companions.

'We've got trouble,' he said quietly to Marty. 'There's that lawman we had our little disagreement with. I'll bet that sonofabitch is looking for us.'

Marty had just finished fastening his cinch; he looked over Lonesome's back.

'Looks like things are likely to get a bit complicated around here. When that lawman gets over the Indian scare I reckon he'll be looking for us.'

'He probably don't know our names,' Harvey said. 'If we keep out of camp as much as possible in daylight hours, he might miss seeing us.'

'I can't figure this out. We found no fresh tracks of any Indians yesterday, and by the way those fellas are riding about on the hill over there they ain't found any tracks either.'

'Could be a single horse thief,' Harvey suggested. 'Remember those Comanche horse raids. They often started without horses – just carrying a rope and a small saddle arrangement that they could stuff with grass when they had a horse to put it on. An Indian on foot is mighty hard to track.'

'I know all that, but if a horse was stolen last night the owner would be kicking up a fuss by now.'

'Just suppose that an Indian saw the chance of an easy scalp and took it in preference to a horse. You know how much they value scalps.'

'That may well be,' Marty admitted. 'But with no means

of escape the scalp hunter would need to have a good place to hide – close by.' They watched from a distance as one of the deputies came back and halted his horse in front of Ransom.

After a brief conversation the rider wheeled his mount away and cantered back up the hill. The wagon boss immediately called to a couple of bystanders and started giving orders liberally laced with profanity. He was arranging the recovery of the dead man's body when he heard a small cough behind him. Turning, he saw the Gilbert sisters wearing identical looks of concern.

'Mr Ransom,' Judy said politely, 'can you please tell us what is going on here?'

'We don't know the full story, Miss Gilbert, but it appears that one of our people was killed last night. Looks like the killer was an Indian. We won't be moving for a while until we are sure that there isn't a war party lurking near by.'

'I thought that the Indians were all gone,' Marjie told him.

'So did I, young lady. We had experienced scouts out yesterday and they saw no recent sign. There's no need to worry; we have enough armed men to stand off any war party and the killing was probably the work of a lone scalphunter. You will be safe here, so try not to worry too much.'

Marjie frowned and looked back over her shoulder in the direction from which they had travelled.

'What about those poor sick men we left behind yesterday?' she asked. 'They would be in no shape to protect themselves.'

Ransom rubbed the back of his hand across his stubbled chin. He had forgotten about Brown's wagon. The ladies had raised a good point and the wagon master, who prided himself on having all situations covered, was momentarily at loss for words. Looking around for inspiration he sighted Marty and Harvey standing by their saddled horses. He pointed to them.

'See those two young fellows over there with their horses? I was just about to see them about that very situation. Come over and I'll introduce you. I'm sure they'll be happy to ride back and check on the men in the wagon. They have good horses and it won't take them long to see how things are and get back to us.'

'Look what's coming.' Harvey chuckled as he saw the three people approaching. 'I knew them girls wouldn't be able to resist us for long.'

'Looks like we must have attracted Ransom too,' Marty observed. 'I wonder what this is all about?'

The wagon boss was a man of few words so the introductions were brief and formal with no first names. But Harvey quickly moved into the opening that they afforded.

'My name's Harvey,' he announced, 'and this is Marty. What can we do for you ladies?'

Marjie indicated her sister. 'She's Judy and I'm Marjory – Marjie for short. We are a bit worried about some sick men that we had to leave behind on the trail yesterday. They had a couple of suspected cholera cases.'

'We heard about that,' Marty replied.

'It was terrible to abandon them like that but it seems there was no other option. We feel that somebody should check on them, and Mr Ransom here thought you boys might ride back and see how they are faring.'

'We ain't doctors,' Harvey said, 'and I sure as heck don't want to get too close to cholera patients, but I reckon we could ride back and maybe do a few things for them if that's possible without taking too much of a risk.'

'There's one risk,' Ransom growled. 'Looks like all the Indians ain't gone yet. That Jennings fella wandered outside the camp last night and got stabbed and scalped for his trouble. Are you sure you didn't miss something yesterday?'

'We scouted our side of the trail yesterday and you had some good men on the other side,' Marty said indignantly. 'There was no fresh Indian sign. The tracks we saw were about a week old.'

Upon hearing about Jennings Harvey immediately thought of Thorpe. He suspected that somehow the latter was involved, but now was neither the time nor the place to start an argument with the law. He saw the lawman riding about on the distant hill where the murdered man had been found, so he discreetly nudged Marty with his elbow.

'I reckon it's a real good idea to go back and check on those poor souls. If they're sick and helpless they don't need a visit from Indians. Let's not waste time, Marty. The sooner we go, the sooner we'll be back.'

'That's very kind of you,' Judy said with a smile. 'But be careful.'

'We always are,' Marty assured her as he swung into his saddle.

Harvey did likewise. 'When we get back we'll let you know how we found things,' he promised.

Marty could see that Thorpe had ceased riding about and had turned his horse back towards the wagons.

'We'd best get going, Harvey, just in case we're needed by them sick fellas.'

Harvey needed no urging. He wheeled his mare around to follow his friend, who was already trotting away from the others.

Thorpe was still fifty yards away when the departing riders caught his attention. The sight of the tall man on the black horse stirred his memory even though he was only seeing his back. There was something familiar about the man on the bay horse too. Recognition dawned.

'Got you – you sonsofbitches!'

CHAPTER 7

Once clear of the camp both riders urged their mounts into a canter. Emma laid back her ears and took a half-hearted snap at Lonesome as she came abreast of him. The riders took little notice as no harm was done and the angry behaviour was more annoying than dangerous.

Marty could not resist a comment.

'Looks like your mare is in one of her mean moods again. She don't exactly have the sweetest disposition.'

Harvey, as he always did, rose to the bait. 'I want a horse, not a wife. She suits me just fine.'

'She's not too bad,' Marty admitted. 'Only trouble is that she's easy to recognize. If Thorpe had an eye for a horse I reckon he might remember where he saw her last – and the long streak of misery on her back could look a mite familiar to him as well.'

'Yes. It's rotten luck that he's still on our trail. I wonder if he's said anything about us to Ransom or some of the others. We might find ourselves in a hornet's nest when we get back to camp.'

'On the other hand we might be able to turn the tables on Thorpe. I don't think it's a coincidence that Jennings happened to get himself killed. Chances are that he knew Thorpe because he was a witness to the killing of Sutcliffe in Lawrence. If Thorpe is still a wanted man he wouldn't want to be recognized.

'You could be right, Marty, but if he's fooled folks about being a proper lawman they might side with him if it comes to a showdown. We don't know for sure how many men we could have against us.'

'Let's forget about Thorpe until we make sure that no Indians have snuck behind us and we see how those sick men are faring.'

They slowed their horses and widened the gap between them, studying the ground for pony tracks and riding wide of places where hostile warriors could conceal themselves. It paid to take seriously any possibility that a war party had doubled back on its tracks.

An hour later they sighted the trees where the wagon had been left, but as they rode closer they could see no sign of it.

At first they thought that they might have the wrong location because they had not been there when the wagon was left, but Ransom had given good directions and they recognized the site of the previous day's noon camp. Marty stood in his stirrups and looked around.

'There's no wagon here,' he said. 'Maybe those sick fellas turned back towards the army roadblock. They couldn't be following the other wagons or we would have seen them.'

Harvey was equally puzzled. He pushed back his hat as if to allow more room for the frown on his forehead.

'They wouldn't be too popular taking cholera cases back to Farrell and the others,' he muttered. 'Let's see what the wagon tracks tell us.'

The tracks only added to the mystery. They showed that the wagon had moved away to the south-west towards a distant patch of stunted trees and a couple of low, rocky hills.

Harvey, when he looked, could discern where the wagon had passed through the sagebrush on the plain.

'Why in tarnation,' he said in a puzzled tone, 'would a

sane man take a wagon into such rough going?'

Marty had a suggestion. 'Maybe he wasn't sane. Could be that the cholera made the driver delirious.'

The pair ceased speculating and turned their horses to follow the wheel tracks. They were no longer relaxed but now fully alert and looking all about them as they rode. Both felt instinctively that something was wrong.

Marty's right hand strayed to his revolver butt while Harvey drew his rifle and held it across his saddle horn. Their search ended unexpectedly.

Fifty yards into the trees they found the wagon smashed to matchwood at the bottom of a deep, rocky erosion gully. One quick glance was enough to see that the three men and the mules were missing.

Riding as close to the crumbling edge as was safe, the pair silently looked down on the wreckage. Neither made any secret of the fact that they were puzzled.

There were no dead mules so the animals could not have bolted and crashed in blind panic; the mystery deepened when the tracks were examined.

The story was plain even if what had brought it about was obscure. The wagon had been partly unloaded, the mules led away and tied to nearby trees. Footprints showed where three men had pushed and levered the wagon over the edge of the gully. It was old and much worn so that the fall on to the rocks had smashed it almost completely.

Marty ventured the opinion that little would be gained by climbing down to examine the wreck. Harvey agreed and dismounted to examine the tracks where the mules had been tied up. The marks in the dirt plainly told the story to men familiar with camp life.

The mules had been saddled, three with riding saddles and two with packs. Footprints on both sides of the pair carrying packs showed that two men had done the loading and securing of the burdens. One other mule had been left free: its hoofprints marked its aimless wanderings as it waited for the men to get mounted.

'Three ridden, two packed and one loose,' Marty observed as he looked around the trampled area.

'It will follow along with the others. Good mules are worth as much as good horses in some places,' Harvey replied. 'If they don't need it, these *hombres* can always sell it somewhere along their way.

'I don't know what game these characters are playing, but they seem to have done a lot of planning and for some reason they are staying away from people. You can bet your boots that the cholera story is a straight-out lie.' He started walking to where they had left their horses ground-tied.

'Those sneaky coyotes ain't all that far ahead of us – a couple of hours. That's all. I reckon we should follow them up even if it's just to tell Ransom and the others what happened here.'

'Good idea,' Marty said enthusiastically. 'We don't want to be back at the wagons too soon with Thorpe hanging around. It's best we take our time and sneak in after dark.'

Cooper was sick of leading the pack mule; he decided to let it free to walk with the two other loose animals.

'Be careful there, Cooper,' Lane warned. 'We don't want to lose that critter. He's carryin' all the money.'

'I know what I'm doing. I'm getting a sore knee from that pack rubbing against it. That mule's well trained. He'll just walk along with us. It's that little hungry-gutted brown one carrying nothing that's the nuisance. He's wandering all over the place grabbing any feed he finds as he goes.'

Kirk turned in his saddle to see that the wayward mule had dropped fifty yards behind them. He was about to go back and chase it up when he saw the animal break into a trot, hurrying to catch up again.

'Don't worry about him,' he said casually. 'He knows

57

what he's doing. It's that black jackass carrying the money that's the important one.'

'He's sure the richest critter in these parts.' Lane chuckled. 'But we know that he's more likely to eat them greenbacks than spend them on whiskey, wild women and cigars. I reckon our money is safe with him.'

That remark touched a raw nerve in Cooper. 'The money's not safe until we do a proper count of it and divide it evenly so that each man carries his own share.'

'Should have done that a week ago,' Lane growled.

Kirk did not disagree but Thorpe's original plan had seemed to be a good one at the time.

'The idea was that we should get well clear of Cedar Flat while Thorpe and the others led the hunt for us in the wrong direction. We had to keep ourselves and the money out of the public eye but until now there's been no chance of us getting clear away. Maybe we can split the loot tonight. There's coins and notes of different sizes all mixed in together. We don't even know how much we really have.'

'It's still the most money we're ever likely to see,' Lane declared. 'When we each have our shares we can split from each other any time we like. One man can lose hisself much easier than three.'

Cooper looked back over his shoulder and saw the brown mule standing still and facing back the way they had come. Something on their back trail had caught its attention. Given the recent Indian depredations in the area, the cautious outlaw halted his mount and faced about. Far away, across the sage-covered plain, he could just discern two tiny moving dots.

'Lane,' he called, 'bring that spyglass you're carrying. There could be someone on our tracks.'

Lane did as he was requested and handed the small brass telescope to his companion, who extended it, cursed his fidgeting mount and eventually located the two riders.

'There's two of 'em,' Cooper said slowly, then cursed as the mule moved again and he lost sight of the strangers.

A short while later he said, 'I've got 'em again. Them coyotes are tracking us. They're riding around following the tracks the loose mules have made. If they weren't tracking they'd be riding straight.'

Lane swore, then asked, 'Do you reckon it's the law?'

'There's no telling at this distance, but we need to find a spot to get them off our trail. No one must know that we are anywhere near here.'

Kirk caught the mule carrying the money and untied its headrope so that he could lead it. Cooper pointed ahead to where a line of cottonwoods, willows and alders marked the course of a creek.

'That's where we can catch them. They're sure to let their horses have a drink and we'll be waiting for them somewhere near by.'

Kirk was not so confident. The plan sounded too simple. 'How do we know they'll cross at the same place?'

'Ain't you got no sense? If we leave good, clear tracks, they'll follow 'em. A muddy creek crossing will show better prints than we leave on grass. While they're having a good look at the tracks they won't be watching for us.'

'Whoever them jaspers are, they're in for a hell of a shock.' The smile on Cooper's face made it plain that he would relish the bloodshed that he was anticipating. 'I'll just have another look in case that pair are scouting ahead for a larger party.' He raised the telescope and squinted through it a while, then lowered it and passed it to Kirk. 'Can't see anyone following. Let's get to that creek and prepare a little reception for them that don't mind their own business.'

Marty steered his horse over to where Harvey was looking at a mule's track. He pointed ahead.

'I just saw something ahead,' he told his partner. 'The sun flashed on something shiny. I reckon someone could be watching us.'

Harvey was at a different angle and did not see the flash but he knew that Marty was a reliable observer. He looked ahead but saw nothing moving among the scattered trees. He frowned.

'Do you think it could be the fellas we're trailing?' he asked quietly. 'I know we're not the only ones out here. It could even be Indians. They use a lot of mirror signals and they'll ride mules if there's nothing else available. Maybe the bodies of those cholera cases are in that arroyo under the wreckage of the wagon.'

'That flash was so quick that it could not have been a signal,' Marty replied. 'Look at the tracks. You can see the men were riding side by side. Indians ride one behind the other so that anyone who finds their tracks has trouble getting an idea of their real numbers. I think that the men we are trailing are closer than we thought.'

'Do you reckon they're watching us?'

'I'll be mighty surprised if they ain't. They must surely have seen us on this open ground if they looked back. Those sneaky coyotes went to a lot of trouble to get away from the wagon train. I reckon they're up to no good.'

'If that's the case,' Harvey drawled, 'messing with them could lead to a few new perforations in our hides. I like mine just the way it is.'

Despite their misgivings they continued on the same course, hoping to see something in the landscape that they could use to their advantage. It was Harvey who first noted that the ground on their right rose gently to a distant crest, where a few mesquite bushes were scattered along the skyline.

'If we change direction slightly,' he said, as he mentally weighed up the situation, 'we'd soon be out of sight.

Anyone watching us will think we've gone in another direction. We could work our way around that high ground, turn south and maybe come in behind anyone waiting to bushwhack us. If they have already moved on, we can easily pick up their tracks again.'

Marty agreed that the idea could work but he still had reservations. He mentioned the possibility of the three men using the same tactics, but in reverse. If that happened both parties would meet head on.

'That's a good reason for us to keep a sharp look out,' Harvey told him. 'We need to see them before they see us.'

Thorpe rode to where Ransom was standing at the tailboard of a wagon that a couple of his men were loading. He had waited for the wagon boss to escort the Gilbert sisters back to where their coach team was being harnessed before he played his next card. The big man wasted no time on small talk.

'Looks like an Indian got that Jennings fellow. He must have been on foot because we couldn't see any tracks. Was probably prowling about hoping to steal a horse but had to settle for a scalp instead. Jennings wasn't very smart to stray from the camp when there was an Indian scare all along the road.'

'I suppose the poor critter figured he was safe. The trail and the campsite had been well scouted. I'll get Ambrose and Happy to have a good look around. If anyone can pick up the killer's tracks they can.'

'That could be a waste of time. Even on foot an Indian can cover a lot of miles in a couple of hours – and tracking a dismounted man in moccasins is slow work. Anyway, I have another problem that's more important to me.'

'What's that?'

'Like I told you before, I'm a special marshal and I'm after some murdering bank robbers. They killed a bank teller while robbing the bank at Cedar Flat, a little town east of here, that's off the main trail. But I'm pretty sure that they headed this way after the robbery.'

The Cedar Flat robbery had been a bloodless affair but Thorpe had learned long ago that people accepted that anyone chasing murderers was regarded as a respectable lawman.

'Do you think they could be with this train?'

Thorpe pretended to think for a while. 'Could be.'

'How many men are you talking about?'

'Nobody's sure of the exact number. Could be as few as two or as many as five. We only have descriptions of two, both in their early twenties, one lanky and riding a black horse, the other somewhere under six feet and riding a bay horse. Both dressed like cowhands.'

'You just missed two men who might be the ones you are after, Marshal. They joined us the day before yesterday. Their names are Redmond and Collins but I've forgotten which is which. They only just rode out of camp. It's a wonder you didn't see them.'

'I recall seeing a couple of riders in the distance but my mind was on other things. An Indian attack this close to our camp does tend to be distracting. I can't recall seeing them around camp. Where were they yesterday?'

'They were scouting the south side of the trail and only came in after dark. By my reckoning they looked a pretty useful pair. Told me they came up from Texas with a trail herd and had never been this far north before.'

'What are they doing today?' Thorpe demanded abruptly. Ransom noted Thorpe's sudden increase of interest.

'They can do whatever they like – this ain't the army,' he replied, 'but they offered to go back to see how things are with them cholera cases we had to leave behind yesterday.'

'I saw the wagon pulled off the main trail. Someone said

it was a sodbuster family.'

'Actually it wasn't a family. It was three single partners expecting to make a new life in the West. I don't like their chances now.'

Thorpe was lost for words for a second or two. The information that three men were involved had suddenly jolted his memory. Then he asked, in a seriously formal manner that concealed his excitement.

'These three men – what did they look like?'

'Fairly ordinary – maybe late thirties or early forties. They kept to themselves Nobody took much notice of them. Them Gilbert ladies were a bit anxious about them so I asked Redmond and Collins to check up on them.'

Thorpe could hardly believe his luck. The five people he most wanted to kill could all be in the one bunch.

'I'll get my deputies,' he said. 'We'll take a little ride back to that wagon, just to see what's going on.'

On Ransom's orders a couple of his men dug a grave while a couple of other volunteers rolled the dead man in his blankets. His mule and a few personal effects were taken by Ransom for delivery to the next town or army post, where proper care could be taken of them.

There was no preacher with the wagons but the boss had buried enough men in his army days to know how to conduct a simple burial service. As soon as the last short prayer was finished Jennings's body was lowered into the grave and men shovelled frantically to fill it in. All were keen to start their journey.

Ambrose was idly riding his pony back and forth, studying the tracks around where the murder had occurred. They had been well and truly trampled and little could be gained from them, so he steered his pony to a patch of long grass to allow it a few mouthfuls while he was waiting.

At first he thought he had seen a small brown animal

hiding in the grass, but it did not flee as he rode closer. His sight was not as keen as it used to be and he leaned down from his pony, expecting to see a dead animal. Then he saw that it was a freshly taken scalp.

There was no mistaking it. Ambrose had seen the results of Indian raids before and had even lifted the hair of a couple of Blackfeet he had killed in his younger days. But his extensive experience immediately told him that a very unusual set of circumstances was involved with this particular trophy.

'Stop shovellin',' he shouted to the men working at the graveside. 'I just found a bit more of Jennings.'

Ransom saw the old man dismount, take something from the ground, remount and ride down the hill toward the camp. As he came closer he saw that Ambrose was enthusiastically waving a scalp.

'Don't fill in that grave yet, boys. I may as well drop this in unless someone wants to keep it.'

Ransom, his face showing his revulsion, looked intently at the grisly object that the scout was holding.

'What do you make of that?' he asked. Ambrose replied in a low tone so as to keep his message from the others.

'It means the late – and probably unlamented – Jennings wasn't killed by an Indian. Someone in this camp did it.'

'What makes you think that?' Ransom asked sharply.

'More than thirty years' experience with Indians has taught me a thing or two about them,' the scout replied, as though addressing a backward child. 'I don't know everything, but keepin' my scalp in place involved a mighty lot of learnin' their likes and dislikes. They are funny about scalps and will often trade good horses to get one. Even if they didn't lift the hair themselves, ownin' a scalp gives a mighty big rise to their social standin'. I can't imagine a warrior goin' to such lengths to get a scalp and then throwin' it away.'

Ransom remained unconvinced. 'Why would a white man go to the trouble to take a scalp and then throw it away?'

'Because he wanted the Indians to get the blame – and you fell for it. Only thing was that he didn't hide that hair well enough. Them bone-headed lawmen trampled out any tracks. The killer threw the scalp into the long grass but he stood off a bit and didn't walk in there for fear of leavin' a trail.'

'Who do you think would be likely to have done this?'

'Don't know.' Ambrose shrugged his shoulders. 'There's round about a hundred strangers here. We don't know half of 'em and I suspect that we mightn't always want to associate with them that we do know. I ain't one of them detective fellers.'

'Don't say anything about this, Ambrose. Just toss the scalp in the grave before it gets too filled in. Let's just blame a stray Indian for the present. When Thorpe comes back I'll have a quiet word with him. He might have some ideas.'

CHAPTER 8

Marty and Harvey breathed a little easier when they crossed over the low ridge that separated them from the men they were trailing. Neither had relished the idea that they might already have been in someone's gunsights.

They saw the creek winding its way southwards, just a couple of inches deep and about two yards across, but frequent bends and a few trees along its banks limited the view downstream.

'Them trees are stopping us from seeing if anyone really is waiting for us lower down the creek,' Marty said in frustration.

'Given the lie of the land they'd be at least half a mile away, if they *are* there. They probably can't see far in this direction anyway.'

'We can see further ahead from here. Let's give our horses a drink and we'll sit in the shade and see if we can spot any movement from where they ought to be.'

Kirk was getting cramped from crouching too long in a patch of tall grass. He knew from the movement of the shadows that enough time had elapsed for the two riders to reach the ambush site, if they were coming that way.

Cooper had arrived at a similar conclusion and waved to Lane, who cautiously stood up and stretched.

Moving warily, the trio came together and conversed in low tones. All were aware that human voices carried a long way on the silent prairie and, with strangers in the vicinity, they needed to be careful.

Kirk lowered the hammer on his Winchester and looked out across the empty plain.

'It don't look like them riders were trackin' us after all. If they were, they would have been here by now,' he said.

Lane was not so sure. 'They drifted over the ridge to the north-west but I'd do the same if I thought I might have been seen,' he told the others. 'They could be workin' their way down the creek towards us.'

'They could be,' Cooper admitted, 'but why would they?'

'Because any white men out here at present are probably from the wagon train. Chances are that they're Thorpe's men. Our little cholera scare might have gained us a few hours but old Jason's not dumb. We need to split that money as quick as we can and then split up our party.'

'Why don't we do it now?' Cooper suggested. 'I'll work up along the creek a bit, just to make sure those riders are gone. If they are we can split the money here. We mightn't get another chance.'

'But what if they're comin' from that direction?' Lane asked.

'There's only two. I reckon I could kill the first one before they know I'm there. If you hear me shoot, one of you holds the money mule and the other comes up to help me.'

Kirk fished a silver dollar from his pocket. 'Heads I look after the money, tails you do,' he said to Lane. 'The loser helps Cooper out if he gets stuck in a fight.'

Thorpe's suspicions were confirmed when he could see no immediate sign of the wagon or its occupants. From a distance a more trusting person might have thought that the sodbusters had simply moved on, but Thorpe's mind was well tuned to criminal thinking. The cholera story had worried him from the time Ransom had revealed the full details.

He set spurs to his horse and rode swiftly to the spot where the quarantined camp was supposed to be. Sanderson and Glasson followed closely.

They halted their horses a few yards from the campsite, having no desire to ride over tracks as they had done at the scene of the Jennings murder.

Glasson was a skilled tracker and he walked his horse slowly forwards, reading the various imprints on the red earth. Sometimes he looked closely at the ground, other times he looked ahead. At last he spoke to his companions.

'Those cowhands that Ransom sent are already on these tracks,' he told them. 'What do we do about them?'

'We get the money first and then we worry about that pair,' Thorpe replied.

'But supposin' they join up with the others,' Sanderson argued. 'We could be up against five guns instead of three.'

'That won't happen. If that pair catch up with Cooper and the others they'll be lucky to survive the meeting. But they might do a bit of damage to our former friends that could slow them down. If any shooting starts we might even hear it. With luck it could reduce the odds against us.'

'So if we hear shooting, we just sit back and wait? Sanderson asked.

'That's right. Odds are that our three former friends will come out on top, but those two cowhands are fairly good with guns and they might cause a few casualties before they go down.'

'Whoever survives won't be expecting us,' Glasson said with a grim smile. 'This will be easier than picking up money off the street.'

They continued their ride, stopping only briefly where their quarry had transferred to mules and disposed of the wagon. The trail was fresh and plain to see so the hunters had no trouble following it at a steady trot. At the place where the two cowhands had split from the trail they paused and looked about.

'Something's wrong,' Thorpe muttered. 'Why the hell did they leave the trail?'

'They're probably trying to loop around and get ahead of Cooper and the others,' Sanderson replied. 'They ain't slowed down by any pack animals.'

Glasson was looking about nervously. He looked long and hard at the distant tree line. 'Maybe,' he said slowly, 'they didn't like sittin' out here in the open like we are, and I don't blame 'em. The sooner we get offa this open ground the better I'll like it.'

'We need to follow those mule tracks, 'Thorpe reminded them. 'Let's pick up the pace and head for those trees.'

Lane was securing the money mule's lead rope to his saddle horn when he thought he heard horses behind him. He noticed too that a couple of the other mules were looking back across the creek. Years of dodging pursuit had sharpened his instincts and cautiously he picked up his rifle before walking back through the trees to get a better view of their backtrail.

Cooper had already mounted his horse and, with his rifle at the ready, rode cautiously through the trees and low shrubs that lined the creek bank. Any attempt to attract his attention would betray their presence, so Lane called softly to Kirk.

'Be careful. I think I hear horses.'

Kirk followed the direction of his friend's glance in time to see three riders threading their way through the trees on the opposite bank.

There was no mistaking the tall, squarely built rider in the lead.

69

In a panic Kirk threw his rifle to his shoulder and fired a hasty shot at Thorpe. The bullet clipped a small twig from a branch that the target had just lowered his head to ride under.

Sanderson reacted immediately. He crashed his horse through some low bushes, drawing a six-gun as he ranged beside Thorpe, who had already vacated his saddle and was using the animal for cover.

Glasson too slipped from his mount, dragged his carbine free and bounded forward. In less than a second he threw a shot at Kirk who had sheltered behind an ancient cottonwood log.

Thorpe and Glasson began firing on their attacker but Sanderson jumped his horse across the narrow stream. He caught a brief glimpse of men and mules before a bullet from Lane's rifle brought his horse down on the muddy edge of the bank. The shooter, however, had not waited around to continue what his instincts told him would be a losing battle.

While the new arrivals were concentrating their fire on Kirk, Lane jumped aboard his mule and, juggling his rifle and the mule's lead rope, kicked his thoroughly frightened mount into action. Momentarily the pack animal hung back on the lead but a graze from a stray shot supplied the incentive for the mule to kick up its heels and start with an enthusiasm that an instant before had been absent.

When Cooper heard the shooting he dragged his mule around and was just in time to see Lane, with the pack mule, bolting from the scene of the fight. He chose to follow the money rather than render assistance to Kirk.

At that moment he saw Marty and Harvey riding through the trees towards him. Convinced that he was caught in a two-pronged attack, he threw a couple of hasty shots in the new arrivals' direction and urged his mule after Lane.

Harvey felt a blow on his lower right leg, which was

thrown back by the impact. Trying to ignore the pain he drew a revolver and sent two angry shots in reply, but distance and hasty aim guaranteed that both missed.

Marty wheeled Lonesome as if to pursue the two riders; he was trying to sight his Winchester on the rearmost of the pair when he became conscious of the gunfight that was continuing further down the creek.

'Are you hit?' he called to Harvey.

'I reckon so. My leg don't feel the best but I can still ride. Do we join in the fight or do we chase that pair?'

'It's best we stay out of this one, Harvey. We don't know what side to take and we need to have a look at that leg of yours. Let's get back into the trees.'

'A good idea,' Harvey said. He holstered his six-shooter and drew his rifle. 'But first I'm gonna show them skunks on the mules that I don't appreciate being shot.'

Cooper had almost caught up with Lane so Harvey delayed his shot until the pair of them together offered a better chance of scoring a hit.

Conscious that being on horseback is impractical for carefully aimed shots, he took quick aim and squeezed the trigger.

The bullet missed both men but thudded into the pack of the already frightened pack mule, which swung violently to the side, breaking its halter in the process. In sheer panic the animal split from the others. The violent change of direction caused the pack to roll under the mule's belly as the saddle had no crupper or breeching. A series of frantic bucks followed before the cinch broke and the animal kicked free and bolted, leaving its load in the sagebrush.

Cooper would have stopped to retrieve the money, but now he found danger from two sources. Thorpe and his men were behind them at the creek and the two unknown riders, who were much closer, could prevent his escape until his former leader finished with Kirk and caught up with him. His mule could never outrun a good horse. Convinced that it was time to cut his losses, Cooper urged his mount after Lane.

Harvey, watching from the sheltering trees, felt that honour had been satisfied and he smiled in grim satisfaction.

'They lost their pack,' he said. 'Serves 'em right. I hope the sonsabitches freeze tonight.'

Marty was not quite as pleased. 'They're still shooting down at the creek bank,' he pointed out. 'We don't know who's who, so let's hide here among the trees, because I have a feeling that we are mighty short of friends around here. If they leave us alone I'll have a look at that leg of yours.'

Kirk was fighting with a determination strengthened by despair and anger. Deserted and outnumbered, he knew that it was only a matter of time before a bullet would find him. Surrender was out of the question: the best he could hope for would be a quick death. If he was wounded and fell alive into Thorpe's hands, his end would be as slow and painful as his former leader could make it.

Sanderson had rolled back down the creek bank to where he could shelter behind the slope and his dead horse. His lower body was in the mud and his boots were in the water but he was well protected. Kirk had to raise himself too high behind his log to get a shot at him.

At best the defensive position could only be temporary because Thorpe and Glasson had abandoned their horses and were creeping, one to the right, and one to the left, to outflank the log barrier.

The fallen tree had a slightly crooked trunk; this, combined with old branches, had held the log off the ground in places. From his low position Sanderson could see the gaps beneath Kirk's shelter. A couple of times he saw his former comrade's feet move past the spaces but they were gone before he could take a shot. Keeping himself concealed, he sighted his gun on the largest of the spaces and waited.

Out to the left, Thorpe had reached a place where he could fire around the end of the log. A couple of shots forced Kirk to move slightly away from his original position and to drop on to the ground to make himself a more difficult target.

Sanderson could scarcely believe his luck when he could see part of Kirk's striped shirt showing through the gap. He fired quickly; as the powder smoke cleared he saw the shirt moving violently. He had scored a hit. Seconds later there was a burst of firing from Thorpe and Glasson. The impact of Sanderson's bullet had rolled Kirk into the open.

'Stop shooting,' Thorpe bellowed. 'We need this bastard alive.'

The order came too late because Glasson had already put another bullet into the wounded man. Kirk, who had struggled to his hands and knees, fell back dead.

Thorpe, in anger, strode across to the fallen man and swore. After exhausting his repertoire of expletives he snarled at Glasson.

'We needed this coyote alive to tell us where the money went.'

'Don't get too mad, Jason,' Sanderson said confidently. 'I saw Lane riding off leading a pack mule. He wouldn't be slowing himself down like that unless there was something special in the pack. You can look out to the open ground and see there are three mules standing together. That brown one has a riding saddle on it, so I reckon it's Kirk's. There's a pack on the chestnut one. If someone rides out there and ropes the pack mule and leads it back here, the others will most likely follow. I'll need the saddled one to replace my horse. While I'm switching saddles, you can go through the pack and see if there's any money there.'

Glasson cantered out to where the mules had started to

graze. He took the lariat from his saddle, deftly roped the pack mule and led it back to the creek bank. The others followed. Sanderson quickly took the one Kirk had been riding and started changing saddles while his companions were eagerly removing the pack.

Their worst fears were quickly confirmed. There was no money among the meagre food supplies and camp gear.

A quick search of Kirk's body revealed only a little small change, which Thorpe threw away in disgust.

'They haven't split the money. You can bet it's on the pack mule they're leading. Which way did they go?'

'I only caught a glimpse of them before my horse was shot,' Sanderson replied. 'They were just disappearing into the trees at the foot of that rocky bluff. You must have seen them.'

'I was too busy with what was going on right here,' Glasson said angrily, 'and I reckon that Thorpe was too. I thought I heard you firing at them.'

'It wasn't me,' Sanderson snarled back at him. Thorpe was not in a mood to argue.

'Get mounted,' he said. 'We'll get on their tracks before they get too big a start.'

CHAPTER 9

Marty and Harvey watched from cover as Thorpe and his men rode out of the trees and set off after Lane and Cooper, who had already disappeared into the brush at the foot of the rocky bluff about half a mile away.

'How's that leg?' Marty asked.

'It's starting to ache like hell below the knee. I seem to feel blood running into my boot but I can wiggle my toes and turn my ankle so I think the bullet missed the bone. Even then it's gonna feel awful sore when it cools down.'

'If you can still ride let's head down to where all that shooting was going on and I'll see if I can find something to patch you up and get you to the wagons.'

'Do you think that's a good idea? Thorpe's likely to head back there sooner or later.'

'You could get blood poisoning if we wait. Patched up properly you might be able to ride still.' Marty turned Lonesome as he spoke. 'As soon as we see what really happened further down the creek I'll try to fix you up; maybe you can get a bit of proper attention back at the wagons.'

'Slow down,' Cooper called to Lane. 'We have to save these mules.'

'To hell with the mules. I'm more interested in saving myself. Thorpe will soon be on our trail. I want to be as far away from him as I can get.'

'We have to be a bit smarter,' Cooper insisted, 'because if we turn this into a race the horses will catch us. Mules are not as fast as horses but they travel well if kept to steady paces. We have to split up and hide. Then, if we give the others the slip, we can double back and try to find the pack that the mule dropped.'

'We might be able to ask that fool critter where it left the pack. Look behind you, Cooper, it's following us. It was probably in double harness with one of the mules we're riding. Seems to me that one of us will have trouble hiding with that loose jackass following. Should I shoot it?'

'No. A shot might bring Thorpe or some of his friends in a hurry. I'll try to drive it away and then try to find some-where to hide. I'll stay around here if I find a safe spot. You can go where you like – but if you give the others the slip, meet me here about noon tomorrow. We can search for the money together.'

'What happens if I don't show up and you find the money?'

'It's your bad luck – and it will mean that you won't be coming. I won't cheat you. If you like you can stay around here and I'll find somewhere else.'

Lane briefly considered the offer but then shook his head.

'This is too close to Thorpe. I'll see you tomorrow.'

Marty and Harvey watched from the trees as Thorpe and his men set out after the two fugitives. Because of the amount of gunfire they heard, the pair were not surprised to see that one man was riding a mule. Horses were big animals and many were hit in close-quarter gun battles.

Marty rode ahead with the butt of his carbine resting on his right thigh. Harvey was a couple of horse lengths behind, trying to ignore the pain in his leg but having little success.

There was no mistaking where the fight had occurred. The dead horse on the creek bank, the dead man a short distance away and the scattered contents of a pack were grim testimony to the violent encounter that had taken place. Kirk was lying on his back staring with sightless eyes at the sky.

'I don't know who this *hombre* is,' Marty dismounted as he spoke, 'but he was probably one of those sodbusters. Someone sure took a dislike to him.'

Harvey was about to dismount when his partner stopped him.

'Stay on your horse. We might have to leave in a hurry and you might not be able to get back on. I can treat that leg from the ground.'

'Since when were you a doctor?'

'As of now. Stop bellyaching and take your foot out of the stirrup so I can get your boot off. I can see what looks like a not-too-dirty shirt over there that someone has pulled out of that pack. I can make bandages out of that.'

Harvey's boot came off easily but the effort required still resulted in a fair amount of pain. Then Marty produced his pocket knife and slit the leg of Harvey's trousers up the side seam to the knee.

'You just wrecked my new pair of pants,' Harvey accused.

'Don't worry. We both left our chaps in Grimmett's wagon. Put yours on when we get back and nobody will know about your damaged pants.'

Marty examined the wound and looked at the hole in the broad stirrup leather. The heavy leather had absorbed some of the bullet's impact before it punched through, struck Harvey's boot top, grazed his lower leg, and went on its way.

'You're lucky, Harvey. That bullet hardly scratched you.'

'If I was lucky the dang thing would have missed altogether.'

When Marty went to get the shirt he had noticed, he saw an almost empty whiskey bottle lying near the pack. Fortunately the cork was still in and there was enough to soak a small piece of torn shirt and use it to clean the wound. The treatment stung but the wounded man gritted his teeth and made no complaint. He knew that, despite his casual approach, Marty was doing the best that he could for him. The improvised bandage made his injury slightly less painful but riding would be far from comfortable.

The boot could not be replaced painlessly and the process was punctuated by sharp intakes of breath and the odd gasp of pain before it was in place again.

Harvey straightened in the saddle and gathered his reins.

'That's fixed. Now where do we go?'

'We go back to the wagons,' Marty told him. 'That leg needs proper attention. It won't get right on its own.'

'Ain't you forgetting about Thorpe and his friends?'

'That is one hell of a problem, but Ransom is supposed to be a square dealer. He might be able to help us when he knows the full story.'

'But what if he doesn't?'

'That's a chance we will have to take.'

Cooper waited till they were riding over a big slab of bare rock before he turned his mule away from Lane and rode carefully into a patch of brush. Anyone on their trail would not see where his mount had changed course. Resisting the urge to hurry, he was careful not to leave tell-tale signs of bent or broken bushes. Eventually he found a spot under an overhanging rock from where he could observe their backtrail and remain concealed.

He had forgotten about the loose mule until he saw it in the distance, trotting along on their tracks. The animal had its nose in the air as if it could scent its old team mate. If it turned into his hiding-place, he would be in trouble for he knew that Thorpe would not be far behind. Anxiously he watched as the mule reached the rocky ground where he had parted with Lane. For a second he held his breath, then relaxed as the mule turned in the direction that Lane had taken.

A short time later Thorpe and his two henchmen appeared on the scene. They were travelling at a fast canter and were concentrating on the clearly visible tracks left by the double-crossers. None of them even glanced in Cooper's direction. There was a fresh trail to follow and there was no indication that the men they sought had parted company.

Cooper watched the trio until they disappeared in the broken ground and cedar thickets. He heard no gunshots and knew that Lane was still keeping ahead of the pursuit. Luck had been with him because the loose mule's tracks had disguised the fact that he had changed direction. That same animal was likely to be Lane's downfall because it would lead Thorpe directly to him. He had not planned the situation but the bright side to it was that he was the only one who knew the approximate location of the lost pack containing the money.

Then his elation disappeared as he remembered the pair of riders whom he had taken to be Thorpe's men. He did not know where they were but suspected that they had been left to guard the money after the pack had been found. He had to get away from where he was but could not afford to run into anyone else, as he would have no friends in that particular slice of territory.

Lane knew he was in deep trouble when the country ahead of him gradually became more open and level. The trees were fewer and the cedar thickets were smaller and more scattered. Because he was unfamiliar with the locality, he had bypassed a couple of possible hiding spots in the hope of finding something better. Now he was in more open country where his sure-footed mule had no advantage over the pursuers' faster horses. If they sighted him, he would quickly be run down.

He was searching for an old buffalo wallow, an erosion gully or some other place of concealment when he heard the distant braying of a mule. Then, before he could move to silence it, his own mule replied. He knew that anyone on his trail would hear the raucous, far-reaching sounds.

In ever-increasing panic Lane turned his mule away and fled. He had no idea of where he was going and would be happy to be anywhere out of his enemies' shooting range. He knew that the type of horse that Thorpe always rode would eventually run down his mule but could only hope that somehow bad luck would strike his pursuers. A horse could fall on the rough ground or go lame. It might have already been tired. If he stuck to rugged country his sure-footed mule might just manage to keep ahead until nightfall.

A rifle shot sounded behind him but Lane knew that the shooter had little chance of scoring a long-range hit. It was merely Thorpe's reminder that he had been sighted and a not-so-subtle hint that retribution was at hand.

Within another half-mile Lane's luck ran out. His mount burst through a screen of low-growing bushes to find itself on the lip of a small gully that had not been visible. The mule propped, then changed its mind and jumped. It cleared the ditch but fell on its knees on the other side.

Lane had just drawn his rifle from the California-style carrying loop on the saddle horn. Almost being thrown when the mule attempted stopping, he was off-balance when the animal suddenly jumped. The landing was not a clean one and as the mule's forelegs buckled, the rider was launched from the saddle. He landed awkwardly, hitting his chin on his knee and bruising his ribs as he rolled on to the rifle. His fear though, transcended his discomfort and Lane jumped to his feet, just in time to see the mule struggle up and trot away.

Thorpe, on a big, brown horse, was within two hundred yards away, brandishing a carbine and yelling in triumph. The other two were about a hundred yards behind Thorpe but were only seconds away. Lane knew then that a snowball in hell probably had better survival prospects than he did.

He snatched up his rifle and rolled into the gully that had been his undoing. The weapon had been ploughed into the soft earth and was covered in grit but there was no time for cleaning it because Thorpe was already at close range. Unfortunately for Lane his bad luck still continued.

He threw his rifle to his shoulder and sighted quickly, only to find that the notch in the rear site was clogged with dirt. With no time to correct the situation, Lane trusted to luck and fired, but the bullet sped wide of the intended target.

The dirt grated in the mechanism as he reloaded but the rifle still fired. The next .44 slug went somewhere into the distance as Thorpe sat his horse back on its haunches and jumped from his saddle. He hit the ground running and, at a couple of yards' range, fired his Spencer carbine from the hip. The big soft lead bullet tore through Lane's shoulder, twisting his body and causing him to drop his weapon and roll back into the ditch.

'Don't do it!' Thorpe shouted as he saw his victim struggling to draw a revolver. He wanted Lane alive but as he levered another cartridge into the Spencer and cocked it again, he saw that the wounded man had succeeded in drawing the weapon. Whether it was intended or just a conditioned reflex, Thorpe fired again, this time shooting Lane in the forehead. The latter collapsed instantly, twitched once and then lay unmoving.

'I thought you wanted this coyote alive,' Glasson remarked as he halted his lathered horse at the scene.

'He left me no choice. When someone draws a gun on me, I shoot to stop them the quickest way I can. We can afford to lose this bit of buzzard meat. Cooper's around here somewhere.'

Sanderson arrived on his mule in time to hear Thorpe's reply.

'Findin' Cooper might not be as easy as you think, Jason,' he said. 'I seem to recall that Cooper was the best tracker in our outfit and he knows how to hide a trail.'

'He can't have gotten far, we can backtrack and see where he turned off.'

'It ain't as easy as that. We rode over their track in places and loose mules complicated things further. Findin' where Cooper turned off is gonna take time.'

'He'll use that time to increase his lead,' Glasson muttered. 'We need to keep a good scare in him. Given time to go a bit slower; mules are good travellers.'

Thorpe thought for a while. 'We'll rest our critters here for the time it takes to search this traitor in case he's carrying important information,' he eventually announced. 'Take anything you want, but I'm taking his spyglass. He sure as hell won't need it. Leave behind any extra weight, like guns, that only add to the load on your mounts. We need to get this skunk if we want to find the money.'

The two cowboys were unfamiliar with the country but knew how to hold a straight course. They turned their horses to the north, where they hoped to intercept the wagon train. It was several hours since they had left it and both knew that it would be somewhere along the trail heading for the next campsite. They were also aware that if they reached the wagons before Thorpe returned they could feed and rest their horses and have Harvey's wound attended to.

They would sound out Ransom in the hope that he might believe their story. Even if he did not, he might be persuaded to stay out of any conflicts that might occur.

A long, low cloud of dust hung in the sky, so the moving train was easy to find. The men turned their horses towards it but had not reached the wagons before a rider emerged from behind a clump of tall cactus, holding a Winchester across the pommel of his saddle. They immediately recognized Ambrose who had been scouting along the left flank of the train.

'Thought it was you two,' the mountain man greeted, 'but I wasn't about to show myself until I was sure.'

'There couldn't be two other fellas this good looking,' Marty said, laughing.

'Thought I might've seen you earlier. Don't tell me you got lost.'

'We struck a bit of trouble,' Harvey replied. 'That cholera story was only a hoax. Them sodbusters left the wagon and set off on mules. We were trailing them when Thorpe, that so-called lawman, turned up and started a gunfight. They killed one of the sodbusters and chased the other two away. There was a lot of lead flying for a while. We kept out of it but I still managed to get shot in the leg.'

'How bad?'

'It could have been worse, but I need to get it patched up.'

Ambrose frowned but offered no sympathy 'Do you know what this is all about? There's somethin' odd and I reckon Thorpe's in the middle of it. That Jennings fella who got killed last night wasn't killed by any Indian. I reckon he was killed by someone from the camp and was scalped to make it look like some lone warrior snuck up and killed him.'

Marty was not convinced. 'How many men in the camp would know how to scalp someone?'

'You'd be surprised, sonny. There were a few guerillas on both sides of the Border War who took scalps as trophies. They were mostly with the Missouri bushwhackers but the Kansas crowd had a few as well. If some of those characters were travelling with us they'd hardly tell us. The law is still lookin' for some of them that were involved in Quantrill's Lawrence raid.'

Marty and Harvey exchanged glances as they thought of Sutcliffe's watch but made no comment.

Harvey complained about the pain in his leg and they took their leave of the scout after warning him to be wary of anyone else approaching from the same direction as they had.

'See Max Kendall when you get to camp,' Ambrose called after them. 'He's drivin' the coach them Gilbert girls are in. He keeps a few bandages and stuff in a box under his seat in case a horse or a passenger gets hurt. Tell him I sent you.'

Harvey turned his horse back and waved in acknowledgment before resuming his journey.

Gus Ransom was more curious than worried as he directed the wagons and lighter vehicles into their defensive positions for the night. He was fairly confident that the Indian threat had moved away but he had heard nothing from those who had ridden out to check the welfare of the suspected cholera sufferers.

Thorpe's attitude troubled the wagon boss too. The lawman had made only a token effort to investigate the murder of Jennings. Instead he seemed more concerned about the identity of the mysterious sodbusters.

There also seemed to be something suspicious about Redmond and Collins. The lawman had implied as much but had not elaborated.

Whatever the problem was, if all went well the wagons

would reach the town of Gopher Creek by tomorrow night. There Ransom's responsibility would end. The travellers would disperse and the wagon boss would resume his normal freighting business, free from the worries of the last few days.

He had already ceased to worry about the missing sod-busters. They were not his problem. The murder of Jennings did worry him, but Ransom was determined to pass that particular buck to the lawmen and then to forget about it.

CHAPTER 10

Marjie was washing dust from her face and hands with a tin dish half-full of creek water that she had placed on the coach's luggage boot. When she heard the horses approaching she looked around to see Marty and Harvey rounding the end of the unharnessed coach. Harvey was slumped in his saddle, obviously in pain, his face set in a grimace.

'Hello, Mr Collins. You don't look well. Is everything all right?'

'I could be better, Miss Gilbert. My leg ain't the best at present.'

'We're looking for Max Kendall, the coach driver,' Marty interrupted. 'Ambrose said he has some medical stuff. Harvey has a bullet wound that needs a bit of patching up.'

'My goodness! That's awful. Mr Kendall's down at the creek watering the team but he once told me that he keeps some medical stuff in an old carpetbag under the driver's seat. If you get it down for me we can see what's in it. How did you get shot, Mr Collins?'

'We were unlucky enough to meet some people who didn't like us,' Harvey told her through gritted teeth. 'It was them sodbusters you were so worried about. For folks dying of cholera they were looking rather healthy – or at least two of them were.'

'What was wrong with the third one?'

'That Thorpe character arrived with his two sidekicks and between them they killed one sodbuster and chased away the other two.'

'So Marshal Thorpe rescued you?'

'He didn't even know we were there. We were staying out of the fight but one of them sodbusters took a shot at me as they were riding away – probably thought we were with Thorpe.'

Marty had dismounted and found the carpetbag covered in dust under the driver's seat. He climbed down with it in his hand. Just then Judy arrived.

'What's happening?' she asked anxiously. 'Is there some sort of trouble?'

'Harvey got himself shot,' Marty replied shortlly as he opened the bag and began examining the contents. 'There's a bottle of liniment here. Do you think that might help?'

'It certainly won't!' Judy was horrified. 'He's not a horse. Liniment would be very painful on an open wound. Is there anything else?'

Marty produced a bottle half-filled with a light-brown liquid. He pulled the cork and sniffed.

'I think it's whiskey, the real rotgut kind. I put some of that on his leg just after he was shot, didn't seem to do him any good. Maybe I should have tipped it down his neck.'

'We can use it to clean the wound,' Marjie said. 'Get him off his horse and sit him on that trunk there. Are there any bandages in that bag?'

'There's two here. They look clean.'

'They'll have to do. Now, quickly, sit him down and get his boot off.'

Harvey was about to dismount unaided but suddenly remembered that the wound was in his right leg, which would be first to take his weight when he stepped down. He took his left foot from the stirrup first and awkwardly slipped from the saddle, clinging to the horse and making sure that his left leg took the shock of landing. For a moment or two he stood there to recover before Marty helped him to a seat on Judy's trunk. He gritted his teeth as his partner eased off his boot and the bloodstained sock.

By this time a small crowd had gathered and Kendall, the driver, returned to the coach. He nodded in approval as Judy cut off a small section of bandage and soaked it in water to clean the wound.

'Put some salt in that water,' an onlooker suggested. 'It helps stop the wound going bad. We used it a lot in the Civil War when we couldn't get help for wounded men.'

That suggestion was met with general approval, so proceedings were halted until a handful of salt was brought from the cook's wagon and mixed into a fresh dish of water that Judy had acquired.

Harvey was far from happy with the unwanted attention he was receiving, and the curious onlookers, after seeing the first phase of the operation, were already asking about what had happened.

The wound was stinging although Marjie was being as gentle as possible. At last she announced that the injury was as clean as she could make it with water and reached for the whiskey bottle to finish the process. But Kendall beat her to it.

The driver took a large gulp and coughed a few times before passing the bottle back to the girl.

'Couldn't let you waste all my emergency liquor on that sort of emergency,' he explained. 'If I die of thirst who will drive the coach?'

The raw liquor burned Harvey's leg; he gasped and complained that it should have all gone to the driver.

Ransom arrived and saw the circus. 'Your friend's in good hands,' he said quietly to Marty. 'Let's get away from here and have a talk.'

They walked a short distance away from the others. When they were safely out of earshot Ransom demanded in a low voice,

'What's going on between you two and Marshal Thorpe?'

Marty explained the situation as he knew it. Ransom listened intently although his impassive face gave no indication of whether he believed what he was hearing. A couple of times he asked for clarification of certain points of the narrative, nodding in silent agreement or sometimes shaking his head with a puzzled or disapproving look.

'There it is,' Marty finished. 'The whole story as we know it. Believe it or not: it's up to you.'

'Now I'll tell you what I think,' Ransom replied. 'I agree with you that Thorpe does not seem to be a genuine law officer. If he is, he is a long way out of his jurisdiction now. It appears as though he was hunting those three sodbusters. If there really was a bank robbery and the manager was murdered, those three might have done it.'

'When he tried to capture Harvey and me he didn't say anything about a bank manager being murdered,' Marty told him. 'We killed one member of his posse when they attacked us for no reason, but that didn't seem to worry him at all. When we took him prisoner he was trying to talk us into coming back with him, but we were not stupid enough to go back to a lynch mob or to be murdered on the trail so he could claim a partial success in his manhunt. He only showed real concern when we took his gold watch as part payment for the loss of our pack outfit. According to what Jennings told Harvey, it was probably stolen anyway.'

'You know that Jennings was murdered last night?'

Marty nodded. 'We do, and we think that Thorpe might have had a hand in it. Jennings warned Harvey to get rid of the watch and he reckoned he knew the story connected with it. He claimed that he saw a man named Sutcliffe murdered and his watch stolen by one of Quantrill's men during the raid on Lawrence, Kansas. Certainly, the name of Thomas Sutcliffe is engraved inside the watch case. Jennings never knew the guerilla's name but the description he gave fits Thorpe.'

'Are you sure of that?'

'No, we're not, but when you connect that watch to both Thorpe *and* Jennings – an eyewitness – a certain picture seems to be coming together. There could be quite a few big, middle-aged men with badly busted noses but Thorpe had Sutcliffe's watch and that sure narrows the field.'

Ransom looked worried. He had looked all around and skywards for inspiration and had found none.

'I have no idea whether or not I should get involved in this,' he admitted. 'I'm not a law officer, just someone who helped organize a bunch of travellers. The trouble is that we are looking at two different situations. Thorpe might be a lawman chasing bandits, and they could be those sod-buster characters. A suspicious person like that marshal could even suspect you and your sidekick of being in cahoots with the other three robbers.

'The second problem is that you and Harvey could be totally innocent but are holding a watch likely to implicate him in a murder committed nine years ago. In either case Thorpe's going to cause a lot of trouble when he comes back here. There could be a lot of innocent people shot.'

'If you don't want to get involved, can I count on you to stay out of any ructions between Harvey and me and

Thorpe?' asked Marty. Ransom answered without hesitation:

'I can only speak for myself but I'll stay out of things as long as I'm uncertain. I have a few more of my wagons with this train and I will tell my men that I don't want them involved. However, if I find out who murdered Jennings I'll take the side that will bring that murderer to justice.'

'Surely you don't think that we had a hand in that,' Marty said in an aggrieved tone.

'Until all the real facts are known I'm not suspecting or supporting anyone.'

Night was falling and Thorpe's frustration was rising. The lowering sun had thrown long shadows across the sage-brush, making it difficult to find the hoofprints of Cooper's mule. The three men were working over ground that had already been crossed by a number of horses and mules. The all-important tracks that would show where Cooper had split from Lane continued to elude them.

Mule hoofs were longer and narrower than those of horses, but the prints the individual animals made appeared remarkably similar to all but the most skilled trackers. The hunters had to find the tracks of a single mule travelling in a different direction and, as the light failed, this was proving to be impossible.

Thorpe knew that Cooper had gained such a long start that he could slow his mule to a fast walk that it could maintain for many hours. In contrast, his own horses had been hard-ridden over the last couple of days and needed rest.

Reluctantly he decided to return to the site on the creek bank where they would supply themselves from the abandoned pack and rest their mounts until the next day.

If Thorpe had been worried before, his anxiety was intensified when they reached the scene of the recent fight.

'Somebody's been here after us,' Glasson said. 'That

pack's been moved. I remember seeing it over there near that log.'

'Do you reckon Cooper might have doubled back?' Sanderson asked.

'He had no need to. He knew that the money was not there,' Thorpe replied. Then a thought struck him. 'We've been forgetting about those two cowhands. They were on those coyotes' tracks too. Where did they get to?'

Glasson suddenly snapped his fingers. 'That's it. Remember I said I thought I heard someone else shooting? It was those two,' he announced with the air of one who had made an important discovery. 'They've been hanging around like buzzards waiting to see what they can pick up.'

The trio looked at each other but it was Sanderson who spoke first.

'Do you reckon they might have found the money?'

'Maybe,' Thorpe said doubtfully. 'But Lane and Cooper took a pack mule with them. They wouldn't have done that if it wasn't carrying the money.'

Sanderson then created another doubt. 'That mule wasn't carryin' any pack when we saw it later. Chances are that someone took off the pack, got the money out and turned the mule loose.'

Thorpe still had his doubts. 'I'm not sure that Cooper and Lane had time for that.'

'Maybe not, but them cowhands might have had time. They could have carried the pack saddle to somewhere safe, took out the money, and vamoosed.'

'We won't know what happened until we find the pack saddle,' Glasson reminded them.

'Or if we find Cooper alive,' Thorpe added ominously.

The discussion continued for several minutes. All agreed that it was too dark to search properly and they decided to camp where they were so as to rest their mounts, and to begin the hunt again at daylight.

Sanderson found some bacon, ship's biscuits and coffee scattered around the abandoned pack. There would be enough for a single, small meal for each of them. When he conveyed the news to Thorpe the big man decided that they would eat later that night to enable a quicker departure in the morning. He wanted to be on the trail before the sun straightened the bent bushes and grass caused by the day's activities.

The next day would be a hungry one but the former guerillas had been used to such privations. Given the choice between money and food they all preferred the former.

Cooper was stretched out on a flat rock looking to the south-east. Darkness had fallen half an hour before but in the last few minutes of light he had seen the distant figures of his former comrades at the site of the gun battle on the creek bank. When the tiny blaze of a campfire suddenly showed in the darkness he knew that his pursuers were stopping for the night.

Tomorrow he would put his plan into action. It was audacious but he was counting on his long experience with Thorpe to succeed. He was a gambler but he reckoned that the odds were slightly in his favour. Thorpe was tricky but Cooper was sure he had seen all of his tricks and could use the knowledge he'd acquired to his advantage.

The night would be long and uncomfortable but Cooper would put the darkness to good use.

The wagons were camped together for the last time. They had stopped at a small creek a few miles short of Gopher Creek township. Some of the more lightly loaded wagons had pushed on, and some of the thirstier single travellers had also ridden ahead now that the Indian scare was over.

Ransom presided over a much smaller camp. He wanted

to keep his teams in good condition, giving them a normal day now and a short day the next. He saw no point in making the trip in one long, arduous day to the detriment of his stock.

For the same reason the coach driver with the Gilbert sisters had also stayed with Ransom, although a couple of his more impatient customers had hitched rides to town.

Harvey was enjoying the attention that Marjie Gilbert was giving him and was in no hurry to leave the camp. His wound had been tended and his dirty socks washed. They were being dried by hanging them on the luggage rail on top of the coach. Kendall, the driver, was not thrilled by the new decorations but he too was smitten with the bright smiles of his female passengers.

Marty came to collect his partner and help him in to a bunk rigged for him in Grimmett's wagon. He was leading Chief, their pack pony.

Judy came from behind the coach, where she had been packing her belongings.

'That's a pretty pony, Marty,' she said. All formality had been dropped by now. It was hard to stay formal with someone who had provided such tender care. In a very rough world, where women were still scarce, neither man had been exposed to much female company but they were gradually relaxing and starting to enjoy it.

'I brought Chief over so that Harvey can get a leg across him and ride him bareback over to Grimmett's wagon,' Marty explained. 'It's easier than carrying him.'

'There's no reason to move him. A couple of our passengers have gone ahead with the light wagons that are aiming to reach Gopher city – or whatever they call the place – tonight. He could travel with us in the coach.'

Marty frowned and shook his head in disagreement. 'That wouldn't be a good idea. There's likely to be a bit of lead flying when a certain skunk named Thorpe gets here.

94

We don't want innocent people getting shot.'

'Are you sure? Why would Marshal Thorpe be shooting at you and Harvey?'

'He might still be following up a false bank-robbery charge against us, or he might be trying to get back Sutcliffe's watch.'

Judy's eyes widened.

'Whose watch?' she asked in a small voice.

CHAPTER 11

Ransom had just finished his evening meal when he saw the group approaching. There were the Gilbert sisters and Marty, who was supporting his very lame partner. The flickering light of the campfire caught the serious expressions on all four faces.

'Is this a social call or are you young folks planning a mutiny?' the wagon boss joked, in an attempt to lighten the mood.

'These ladies have some important information that we reckon you should hear,' Marty answered. 'It's about the man calling himself Marshal Thorpe.'

Ransom rose from his seat on the wagon tongue and stepped closer to the sisters.

'You have my undivided attention,' he said. 'Please go ahead.'

Marjie looked him in the eye. 'Did Marty tell you about the gold watch that he and Harvey took from Thorpe?' she asked.

'Yes.'

'Did he tell you about the name inscribed on the watch?'

'Yes. It was Sutton or some name like that.'

'It was Sutcliffe,' Marjie corrected. 'Thomas Sutcliffe'.

'So what does that have to do with me?'

'Sutcliffe was our mother's maiden name,' Judy inter-jected. 'Her brother was Thomas Sutcliffe, who was very active on the Kansas side of the Border War. He was mur-dered by Quantrill's men when they raided Lawrence, Kansas in 'sixty-three. The killer took his gold watch as a trophy. As children we heard the story several times from the Sutcliffe side of the family. The murderer was a big man with a badly broken nose. Some say his name was Thornhill but no one was ever really sure.'

'So you reckon maybe this Thornhill, calling himself Thorpe, killed your uncle?'

'The description fits and he would be about the right age,' Marjie said in a confident tone of voice. 'Seeing as he had Uncle Tom's watch, I can't think of a more likely suspect.'

'Does anyone know what happened to this Thornhill character?'

'We were only children. The adults did not tell us any of the real details, but from somewhere I heard that the law was after him. As far as I know they never caught him.'

Marty joined the conversation. 'We never heard of him in Texas. A heap of bad men headed that way after the war. Much of it is close to the Mexican border and a lot of shady characters drifted there. Some old Confederates tried to join the French side when they were in Mexico fighting the Juaristas. Many of these never made it back home.'

'Don't I know it,' Ransom said ruefully. 'I was one of the lucky ones who did.'

'You would know then how easy it was for a wanted man to disappear into Mexico and then turn up a couple of years later in Texas or Arizona with a new name,' Marty con-tinued.

'I agree with you there, Marty. In recent times I have seen quite a few old familiar faces with names their parents never gave them.'

'And it ain't a long stretch from Thornhill to Thorpe,' Harvey remarked.

The wagon boss tugged at his short beard for a while before giving his well-considered reply:

'I reckon that Marshal Thorpe is more likely to be a murderer named Thornhill than that you two boys are murdering bank-robbers. I have half a dozen or so good men with my wagons here who will back you if that fake lawman comes after you, but I want to avoid any unnecessary killing of innocent parties who might be camped with us. If Thorpe wants to ride away, I'll let him rather than have a gun fight in the camp. If all goes well, we can see Sheriff Kelner in Gopher Creek tomorrow and try to come to some sort of an arrangement with him. How does that sit with you fellas?'

The two partners agreed to the proposal but Harvey added one condition:

'We agree as long as you also guarantee to raise the matter of Thorpe with any genuine lawmen you cross paths with.'

'Suits me – but will you to do the same?'

'We will if we get the chance,' Marty told him. 'But we're Montana-bound and will soon be out of this territory.'

Cooper had spent an uncomfortable night but was reasonably satisfied. He had found the hiding-place he sought, as close to his hunters as he dared to go. Years of dodging army patrols and posses had taught him that most searchers, on breaking camp, would hurry to where they had lost the tracks on the previous day. In his case, that point was nearly two miles from where they were camped. He had staked his mule, already saddled, in a patch of brush further up the creek, well away from where he calculated that the search area would be.

Rifle in hand, he crept to a clump of greasewood bushes

just tall enough to conceal him when he stretched himself flat on the ground. Through small gaps in the foliage he could observe Thorpe and his men less than two hundred paces away. They were working quickly in the early morning light, as if eager to leave the scene of Kirk's death.

Cooper smiled to himself when he saw the mules that had been turned loose. They had wandered around the area all night, grazing on scattered patches of grass and visiting the stream to drink. In the process the animals had made new tracks and trampled over some of those from the previous day. The morning sunlight would begin to straighten bent bushes and grass, so Thorpe and his sidekicks would have no easy task in locating the tracks they needed to follow.

They acted as Cooper had hoped, leaving their overnight camp and riding away out of sight behind some undulating ground where they had lost the tracks the evening before.

Cooper hurried back to his mule. He figured that he might have an hour or so to find where the pack saddle had fallen.

The wagon camp started breaking up early. Many of the travellers were sick of being confined in the crowded camp and looked forward to being the masters of their own destiny again. Some did not even wait for breakfast.

The little single-street town of Gopher Creek had suddenly become a desired destination. It had a saloon, a couple of shops, a hotel and a post office. There were even a sheriff and a doctor. Some travellers would rest there while others would re-supply and hurry through in an effort to make up for some of the time they had lost.

Marty, Ransom and Ambrose rode to town together while the wagons were still being loaded and the teams harnessed. Harvey's leg was sore, so he would travel in the coach with the ladies.

Eastbound travellers were leaving the town in scattered groups, eagerly taking to the road after the monotony of confinement in a small town.

Ransom questioned a single rider towing a reluctant pack mule behind him. Between grunts and curses at the mule the rider confirmed that the telegraph was in normal operation again and that the Indian scare was over.

'It's hard to imagine,' the wagon boss said, 'that a few Indians could cut the entire country's most advanced communications.'

'I still have trouble understanding how sounds can travel along thousands of miles of wire in one day,' Marty admitted. Ransom pointed ahead to a low adobe building on the left side of the road.

'There's Kelner, the sheriff. He's a gloomy sort of customer at any time and won't be exactly laughing when he hears our news.'

Sheriff Bolivar 'Bullseye' Kelner leaned his spare frame against a veranda post in front of his office and looked with disapproval upon the influx of visitors. A hundred armed civilians hitting the town within twenty-four hours was a recipe for trouble. Without the sawn-off shotgun in the crook of his right arm, he would have appeared as just another gaunt, middle-aged man with grey hair and a lined face set in a scowl. The old mountain man chuckled as he saw the lawman.

'Looks like Bullseye's still on the right side of the grass,' he said to Marty. 'He don't look too pleased to see us, though.'

'He'll be even less pleased when he hears our news,' Ransom said in a serious tone.

Marty's curiosity got the better of him. 'Where did he get the name of Bullseye?' he asked.

'It seems that everyone likes to shoot at him,' Ransom

explained. 'He has a Ute arrow head still inside him some-where; he was wounded a couple of times during the Civil War and a few bad actors have managed to put lead into him in various places since then. He used to be pretty fast with a six-shooter but a shoulder wound slowed him down. That's why he always carries that shotgun – his gun is already in his hand.'

'Maybe it's time for him to think of another career.'

Ransom disagreed. 'Bullseye is a mighty good lawman and has lived by the gun for years. He's slowing down and I think he knows that he could be living on borrowed time. He won't change his ways now. He'll play out the hand that's been dealt to him.'

Ambrose sighted the saloon on the other side of the street. Declaring that thirst was killing him, he trotted his horse away from the other two.

'The sheriff don't look too busy,' Marty observed. 'Now might be a good time to ask him what he knows about Thorpe.'

Bullseye straightened up when he saw Ransom and Marty dismount and hitch their horses to the rail in front of his office. No welcoming smile crossed his features although he had known Ransom for several years. He eyed Marty coldly but at least gave a firm handshake when the wagon boss introduced him.

'You look like something's worrying you, Gus,' the lawman said. 'Better come into the office and tell me the bad news.'

The inside of the office contained a battered desk, a couple of closets and a few rickety chairs. A solid but open door at the back of the room led to a corridor between four iron-barred cells, which the visitors could see were all empty.

Bullseye indicated a couple of chairs and seated himself behind the desk. Then, in a gruff voice he spoke.

'I can see this ain't a social call,' he said. 'Something's bothering you, Gus, so spit it out.'

Ransom started to describe the circumstances surrounding the murder of Jennings but Bullseye interrupted.

'I already heard about that. Some of your crowd came into town last night. By now most of the townspeople would know too.'

'That's only part of it,' Marty told him. 'There was another killing yesterday on that little creek about ten miles from here and my partner was shot and wounded.'

'Do you know who did it?'

'It might have been one of three sodbusters who left the wagon train because of a supposed cholera scare.'

'Just hold on there,' said Bullseye. 'This is getting complicated. I'll need to start taking notes.'

The sheriff opened a desk drawer and produced a several sheets of writing paper and a pencil. He hated paperwork and made no effort to conceal the fact. Barking questions, grunting as though physically exhausted, and occasionally crossing out mistakes, he attacked the task as though it was a mortal enemy.

Nearly an hour later he threw down the pencil and arranged his notes in order. After reading them aloud he demanded, in a challenging tone:

'Are you both agreed about this?'

'What about this Thorpe character and that bank robbery at Cedar Flat?' Marty asked.

'Cedar Flat is a long way out of my jurisdiction. I have never been there and have no desire to go there. I know nothing about any bank robbery but, as you know, mail- and stagecoaches were both stopped and the main trail closed when the telegraph system was cut in half.

'But getting back to Thorpe, he sounds a bit suspicious from what I have heard. If you and your friend were his main suspects why would he go chasing after someone else?'

'Could be that he's trying to grab the first people handy. He had no reason to go chasing after me and Harvey and he wasn't interested in taking us alive. He would never have found the stolen money because we didn't have it.'

In all his decades as a lawman Bullseye had gained quite an insight into the minds of criminals. He considered for a moment or two.

'He's after the money,' he said slowly. 'You can bet your boots that those so-called sodbusters were dodging him when they left the wagon train. Thorpe probably knew that you couldn't steer him to the money. That's why he hasn't come back here hot-foot to arrest you.'

'What about the murder of Jennings?' Ransom prompted.

'Doggone it, Gus,' Bullseye growled. 'One crime at a time. I ain't forgotten. I can't be in two places at once. My first job is to go out to where that latest killing took place and see what I can find.

'You might need me too,' Marty said.

'I was coming to that,' the sheriff snapped. He drew a watch from his vest pocket. 'If you can't come I'll have to find some of our locals who know the area. If you can come, make sure your horse is fit for a long ride and bring a blanket in case we have to stay overnight somewhere. Get going now and I'll see you here in about an hour.'

'Do you think two of us are enough? Seems to me that those *hombres* ain't overloaded with peaceful intentions.'

'They won't be there because there's no reason to hang around. They'll be long gone but we might get an idea of what they've been up to and where they're headed.'

Marty stood up. 'I'll just tell Harvey what's happening. I'll be back here shortly. What about grub?'

'I'll fix that,' Bullseye said impatiently. 'We won't need much. Now get going.'

*

Cooper remained in hiding until Thorpe and the others were lost to view behind the ridge. He noted with great satisfaction that the loose mules had hung around where there was grass and water and had added their tracks to those of his own mount. The hunters would have a nearly impossible task in tracking him.

He rode out into the open and began to search for the missing pack. He remembered that it had fallen into a patch of sage that had covered a large area. There had been no time to note any possible landmarks but Cooper was confident that he would be able to locate the money fairly quickly.

It was dangerous to stay in the open country too long and he gambled that Thorpe would be moving away from the area, hoping to find tracks away from the trampled ground.

He was hungry and the warm morning was making him thirsty, but he knew that Gopher Creek township was not far away to the north-west. He promised himself that when he had found the money he would go there and have a decent meal. He was a stranger to the area and recognition was unlikely.

An hour later Cooper still had not found the money and was becoming increasingly nervous. Once, early in the search, he had ridden close to the pack but it was in a thick patch of sage and partly hidden by the long morning shadows. He knew that his hunters had ridden through the same general area and likely would have found the pack if it was there.

The reality was, though, that earlier the shadows had been even darker and his former comrades had been looking for a man, not a pack.

By widening the search area Cooper had unwittingly moved away from his goal. His fears were growing by the minute and he kept glancing at the higher ground to the west. He expected that Thorpe would come from that direction if he found a trail he could follow. For all Cooper knew, his former friends might have extended the search and proceeded to Gopher Creek, but they could also be still searching in the near vicinity.

It was getting towards noon when he spotted movement among the mesquite that lined the crest of the western ridge. Caught in the open, Cooper was looking for a place to hide but then he saw the four stray mules emerge. They were calmly making their way to the creek. Relief flooded through him but he realized that he was trembling violently. Gradually his fear subsided and he told himself that he was lucky. Every time the mules came in to drink. they covered the old tracks, making more trouble for anyone trying to trail him.

Cooper had relaxed too soon because his own mount, upon seeing its mates from the team, suddenly brayed. Immediately its harness partner brayed back. If the hunters were in the vicinity they would hear it.

They did.

Thorpe had given up the search and decided not to waste any more time. He reasoned that Cooper, being unfamiliar with the area, would make for Gopher Creek to obtain supplies and possibly get directions. He and his men would do the same, but first they would go back to the creek for water. Men and animals were thirsty and would travel better after a drink.

'Stupid jackasses,' Glasson said when he heard the first mule. 'Look at 'em standin' on the ridge like they ain't figured out what to do next.'

Then they heard Cooper's mule reply. Thorpe halted his horse and raised a hand for silence.

'How many mules can you see on that ridge?'

'Four,' Glasson replied. Sanderson saw the way their

leader's mind was working.

'That second one was a way off, probably down near the creek. It could be Cooper's, There's four on the ridge and I'm riding one. We know there were only six mules.'

'That's what I'm thinking,' Thorpe told them. 'But is Cooper with it?'

'There's only one way to find out,' Glasson said eagerly. 'If Cooper is with that mule, we can soon corral that back-stabbin' polecat.'

Thorpe touched his horse lightly with the spurs.

'Get a move on,' he called to his men. 'Remember, though. We want this sneaky coyote alive.'

Marty and Bullseye heard the mules braying and halted briefly to listen.

'Those would be the sodbusters' mules,' the cowboy said quietly. 'They're running loose near the creek.'

'It won't take them long to go wild,' the marshal muttered. 'They get cunning, too. Good luck to anyone who can round those critters up.'

Marty had an idea, but all aspects of it had yet to be explored. 'How would the law treat anyone who could catch them?'

'If they're branded they have to be handed in and I need to make an effort to find the owner. That can be more trouble than the mules are worth, but if they're cleanskins, anyone who catches them can have them.'

They were about to continue their journey when Marty spoke urgently.

'Don't move. Let's wait in the trees for a while. There's a rider just come out of the timber near the creek. He's coming this way and he's in a hurry.'

Bullseye drew his shotgun from its loop on his saddle horn. 'Move a bit more to the left, Marty and make sure he doesn't get past us. I want to ask that fellow a few questions.'

Marty pointed towards the ridge on their right. 'There're riders just coming over that hill,' he said. 'Could be they want to do the same.'

CHAPTER 12

Cooper had given way to panic. Aware that his mule's bray might have alerted his hunters, he needed to find a hiding-place. He could always continue his search if it proved that he was responding to a false alarm. A glance to his left showed three riders descending from the ridge about a quarter of a mile away. Even at that distance, he knew who they would be and his blood seemed to freeze.

Cooper had been only half brave in the company of others but now, alone, panic took over.

He lashed his mount with the rein ends and drove in his heels. The mule gave a startled jump but then caught some of its rider's fears and lunged into a gallop. The closest cover was only about a hundred paces ahead but Cooper knew he had been seen and hiding was out of the question. Once in open country the pursuers' horses would quickly run down the mule.

With no other option Cooper started to look around for a position where he might be able to fight off his attackers.

He risked a glance behind him and saw the hunters riding hard on his trail. Looking forward once more, he was shocked to see two riders approaching from that direction. They were only a few yards away. Bullseye had drawn his shotgun.

'Stop!' he bellowed. 'Stop, damn you! Stop!'

Cooper's intentions were never apparent because his

mule almost collided with the sheriff's horse as it tried to force its way through the brush.

Bullseye did not shoot but swung the butt of the gun into the fleeing man's face. Cooper rolled backwards over the mule's rump and hit the ground, stunned.

'Get his gun and watch him,' the sheriff ordered Marty. 'There's more trouble on the way.'

Like lightning, Marty was out of the saddle, drawing his Winchester from its scabbard as his feet hit the ground. Two strides took him to where Cooper, wild-eyed with terror, was about to struggle to his feet.

Finding the carbine's muzzle inches from his face stopped his movements quicker than any verbal command: he obeyed instantly when Marty barked,

'Get on your belly and stay there. One wrong move and you're dead.'

Cooper complied and his captor relieved him of the six-shooter he was carrying.

Thorpe and his men were about a hundred yards away; their surprise at being suddenly confronted by armed men caused much hauling on reins. No one wanted to come into range of Bullseye's shotgun. The sight of Marty dismounted and covering them with his Winchester also caused them to rethink their plans. A man on the ground with a good repeating rifle could shoot more accurately at that range than three mounted men with revolvers.

Thorpe lifted an empty right hand to indicate peaceful intentions.

'Hold your fire,' he called out. 'I'm a law officer.'

'So am I,' Bullseye replied in a tone that indicated that he was not impressed.

'That man's a murdering bank robber.'

'All the more reason for me to take him in. I'm taking him to Gopher Creek and I intend to hold him there until I can check on what's been happening with Ransom's wagon train. You can come into town and state your case if you want to.'

'Fine. We'll go with you just to make sure he doesn't get away.'

'Like hell you will. I don't know who you are, so keep right away from us. I don't want to see you again this side of town. If you come within sight of us, we'll shoot.'

'But I'm a properly accredited marshal with two properly sworn deputies. My name's Jason Thorpe.'

'That should be easy to prove now the telegraph's working again. If I don't see you in town I don't want to see you around these parts again.'

'That man you're holding is very dangerous. You might need some help with him,' Thorpe protested.

'I can be dangerous myself and I'll shoot him dead at the first sign of trouble from either him or you. Now back away, or come in shooting.'

Harvey was restless. Properly bandaged, his leg was not quite as sore. He was wearing clean socks and Marjie had loaned him a couple of safety pins to close the split in the leg of his pants. With his chaps fastened over the damage and his boot in place, he felt the urge to climb back into his saddle and, hopefully, catch up with Marty and the sheriff.

He quickly dismissed any ideas of riding that day when he tried to limp to where his mare was tethered along with Chief and their pack. Grimmett's wagon was moving on and this would leave them to their own devices. He was sitting on his bedroll when the Gilbert sisters walked over to him. His spirits fell when he was sure that they had come to say goodbye. In the short time he had known them he had greatly enjoyed their company.

'We thought you would be going with Mr. Ransom's wagons,' Marjie said, as if pleasantly surprised.

'Marty and me only joined them when the Indian scare

was on. They're headed south to Santa Fe. That's the wrong direction for us, but ain't you going on the coach?'

Judy looked slightly embarrassed. 'We'll be staying here for a while,' she said. 'Coach travel is very expensive and we need to earn a bit more for the next part of our journey. Mrs Mooney at the hotel has offered us work, waiting on tables and generally helping around the place. At least we will have a roof over our heads while we try to scrape together some more money. Eventually we hope to reach Virginia City.'

'How long will you two be staying around?' Marjie asked Harvey.

'Depends on this leg. It's a lot better, but if I ride too soon it could get worse again. There's a heap of riding ahead of us yet.'

'Will you be staying in town?' Judy trusted that she did not sound too hopeful.

'Most likely, unless Bullseye has some local rule about camping down by the creek. Him and Marty are out to have a look around where them cholera cases of yours fell out with that Thorpe fella who claims to be a lawman.'

'What happened to those men?' Judy asked in a puzzled tone.

Harvey moved his wounded leg to a more comfortable position.

'We know for sure one of them's dead,' he replied. 'Maybe all three by now.'

Bullseye wasted no time. Despite Cooper's protestations of innocence he produced a pair of handcuffs from a large side pocket of his coat and tossed them to Marty.

'Put these on our friend, but be careful. Feel free to shoot him if he resists.'

Cooper offered no physical resistance but complained loudly.

'You can't do this to me, Sheriff. I haven't broken any law.'

'What's your name?'

'Brown, Bill Brown. You have to believe me, Sheriff. Those men are road agents. They've already killed my two partners.'

'Good. You can be a witness for the prosecution when I round them up later. But right now you're my prisoner. Keep an eye on him, Marty.'

Marty unfastened his lariat and flipped a small noose over the prisoner's head, allowed a couple of yards' length then hitched the rest of the rope around his saddle horn.

'Be careful,' he warned. 'Lonesome's a mighty good roping horse. If you pull back against the rope, he'll pull it tight again. I reckon he's stronger than you are and if he gets a scare he might drag you a long way before he stops. You'd best do everything I tell you to – and do it quick.'

Bullseye knew that his prisoner was secure and concentrated on the three riders who had retreated to long range for Winchester carbines but had not left the scene. They were weighing their options and the sheriff knew that their intentions were unlikely to be friendly or legal.

'You have to let me go,' Cooper whined. 'They're after me. They'll kill you if you get in their way. Give me one of your horses and I'll lead them away from you. You won't get back to wherever it is you intend to take me. These men are killers. They've already killed my two partners. Give me a horse and they won't bother about you. If you won't do that, give me a gun so I can help fight them off.'

'Why is it that they want you so bad?' Marty asked. Cooper had a well-rehearsed reply in anticipation of that question.

'It's about a gold mine in Nevada. Me and my partners had teamed up to find it. Kirk was the only one who knew where it was. Somehow Thorpe and his men found out about us and friends warned us that they were on our trail. We thought we'd given them the slip until we were held up by that army road block. We knew they'd catch up with us so we changed to our emergency plan and got rid of the wagon. It was too late, though. The murdering polecats tracked us down—'

'They're waiting just out of range trying to figure out how to get hold of our friend here,' Bullseye interrupted. 'They mightn't be so keen on a fight now but I don't want them stalking us all the way back to Gopher Creek.' He turned to Marty. 'This shot-up shoulder of mine affects my rifle shooting considerably. Do you reckon you could land a warning shot near them?'

'It's long range for a Winchester, but if I aim a bit high I should be able to drop a shot near enough. Just keep an eye on this character we have here. I'll get you to hold my horse when I get off so he don't run away with Mr Brown.'

Thorpe's horse shied sideways as a bullet kicked up a spray of dirt a couple of feet in front of it. Almost unseated, the rider grabbed the saddle horn and struggled to retain his balance. Marty chuckled and turned to Bullseye.

'Do you want me to send him another warnin'?'

'Let's see if he took any notice of the one he just got. He's yelling something but he's too far away for us to hear what he's saying.'

'We can hear cuss words any time,' Marty remarked with a broad smile on his face. 'They've split apart and are moving back. Looks to me like they took the hint.'

The sheriff took a notebook and pencil from his coat pocket, scribbled a few words and tore out the page. Then, holding the paper aloft, he waved it to attract Thorpe's attention and jammed it into the fork of a nearby mesquite bush.

'Just in case Thorpe is a genuine lawman and has the right credentials,' he told the others, 'I've officially told

113

him where to find me and our friend here. He can come in alone and we will talk things out. Now, let's get mounted and head for Gopher Creek. I'll take the prisoner. I want you to watch our backtrail. Be careful too that they don't get around us and set an ambush.'

CHAPTER 13

Thorpe read the note that Bullseye had left and his face reddened with rage. He had almost exhausted his considerable stock of profanity and obscenity by the time he'd regained control of his anger. He had the numbers, so the odds in a gun fight were good, but if Cooper was killed in the crossfire they would never find where he had hidden the loot from the bank robbery.

Marty's warning shot had been a fluke but it kicked up the dust close enough to Thorpe to make him wary of closing the distance between them.

'That coyote seems to have the range figured out just right,' Glasson said casually. 'I reckon we should steer clear of him where there's so much open ground and only move closer when we have a bit more cover.'

Thorpe saw the logic in his henchman's suggestion. Though unfamiliar with the country he had seen timber-covered mountains and areas of huge boulders ahead, If they could somehow get around their quarry they might be able to set an ambush.

'They can't travel fast,' Glasson said. 'Cooper lost his mule so he'll either have to walk or ride double with someone. That will slow down the horse concerned. We can travel a lot faster.'

Half a mile ahead the same notion came to Bullseye. Marty had dropped back to watch for pursuers after passing

115

Cooper's neck rope to the sheriff. Complaining loudly, the prisoner was forced to keep pace beside the lawman's fast-walking horse.

'I can't walk this fast,' he protested.

'You'd better learn quick,' Bullseye growled, 'because I don't intend to put any extra strain on this horse. I've been shot in the leg twice and I don't walk too well.'

'You won't be walking too well at all when Thorpe catches up with us. At least give me a gun. You know he intends to kill us all.'

'Folks should know by now that I ain't all that easy to kill. I've handled men like Thorpe before. He don't scare me.'

Actually, Thorpe scared Bullseye greatly, but he had to maintain the façade of self-confidence. Thanks to age, old wounds and arthritis, he was no longer the skilled gunman that he had once been. He could conceal his weakness with those who knew his reputation but a determined stranger might not be so easy to bluff.

So far Marty had shaped up well and the lawman could only hope that the younger man had the skills and deter-mination needed in the confrontation that looked inevitable.

A sudden crashing in the brush behind them sent jolts of fear through both Bullseye and Cooper, but they relaxed when they heard Marty's voice.

'Wait a second. I've found Brown's mule.'

Much relieved, they waited until Marty emerged from the mesquite, leading the missing animal.

'I found this jackass feeding on a patch of grass when I was looking for Thorpe and his crew. We'll be able to move a lot faster now.'

Bullseye wasted no time in transferring the prisoner to the mule. Because they were going into rough country he removed the neck rope but drew his shotgun.

'Ride ahead of me and I'll tell you what directions to

turn. Listen well to what I say because I'll give you a load of buckshot at the merest hint of a wrong move. Now, get going straight ahead.'

'I'll drop back to make sure we ain't being followed too closely,' Marty said. 'If I find them on our tracks I'll fire a warning shot. If they fire back I'll try to delay them enough to give you a good start.'

Bullseye grunted in approval, then added, 'Five minutes – or maybe ten – will give us a good start. Don't do some-thin' stupid like gettin' yourself killed.'

As he watched the others ride away Marty was deter-mined to follow the sheriff's final instructions.

The contingency plan turned out to be a wise precaution because Thorpe and his men were working as quickly as they could through the brush to the right of Bullseye's trail. They intended to move swiftly in a wide arc that bypassed the sheriff's party. Then, because they did not know the country, they would move back towards the incoming tracks and set their trap at a suitable spot. Their reasoning was that the lawman would return to Gopher Creek on his orig-inal tracks.

The idea nearly worked, but an old landslide and a tangle of fallen trees barred their way; to get around it they had to return to the main trail.

It was there that Marty spotted them. He had seen the landslide on the outward journey from Gopher Creek and knew that the point where the canyon narrowed was ideal for a rearguard action.

He eased Lonesome into some chaparral on the slope overlooking the trail and dismounted. He drew his carbine from the saddle scabbard, readjusted the rear sight for close-range work and peered through the concealing foliage.

A large granite boulder stood by the side of the narrow trail and Marty sighted his carbine on that as the three riders approached it. Thorpe was in the lead, peering at the fresh tracks he was following.

Marty fired at the rock and heard the ricochet as the bullet whined off into the trees.

'Stop there!' he shouted.

For a brief moment Thorpe considered charging forward but Sanderson yelled to him to take cover. It would have been suicide to ride into thick brush where two men with repeating rifles could be waiting.

Glasson had seen powder smoke rising from the chaparral; he snapped a couple of shots into the general direction of the hidden rifleman but neither went near their intended target. Their only effect was to warn Marty that the trio had no peaceful intentions.

'Stop wasting lead and get under cover,' Thorpe called. He set the example by wheeling his horse behind a cluster of large boulders. He was securing his mount to a low-hanging pine branch when Glasson joined him.

'Where's Sanderson?' Thorpe demanded.

'He's on the slope across the trail. I reckon he'll be workin' his way closer on foot. We need to keep them lawmen busy to give him a chance to surprise them.'

Of the flurry of activity Marty only had brief glimpses through the trees that concealed him. He saw horses and riders disappearing into the rocks and assumed that all were together.

A few probing shots started landing near by. He saw them clip bunches of leaves from trees and heard others striking the ground or whining away when they hit rock.

There was the distinctive bark of the Winchester and the deeper report of Thorpe's Spencer repeater. A cloud of powder smoke hung low in the trees but it was too scattered to indicate clearly the positions of the shooters.

Marty held his fire. He had secured Lonesome near by in a protected position and was determined not to chance revealing his own location until he was presented with targets.

Sanderson had also left his mule concealed; he stole forward a few paces at a time. In places there were trees but a fairly open area covered with low chaparral was between him and where he knew he needed to go. It would take him a while to crawl through the low bushes, but when it came to manhunting Sanderson was very patient.

'Harvey Collins, just where do you think you're going?' Judy's voice surprised Harvey with its authority.

He paused in his efforts to climb aboard Emma from the edge of a raised boardwalk. 'Just going for a bit of a ride to test out this sore leg. Thought I might ride out and meet Marty and Bullseye. They should be on their way back by now.'

'You shouldn't be riding yet. Why do I get the idea that you're about to do something stupid?'

Harvey eased his right leg across the mare's back and settled carefully into the saddle. As his feet found the stirrups, he said dismissively,

'I'll be fine. I'm just going for a ride. There's no need to worry.'

Before Judy could think of a suitable reply he had wheeled Emma, touched her lightly with the spurs and cantered away.

Bullseye heard the gunfire behind them and hurried with his prisoner along the trail to Gopher Creek. Marty was buying time for them but he expected that the firing would soon end as the cowboy made his getaway. The sheriff had hoped that the pursuers might have sustained some loss and been suitably discouraged, but the continuing sporadic fire convinced him otherwise.

'You're lookin' a bit worried there,' Cooper told

Bullseye. 'That *hombre* you left behind won't hold Thorpe up for long. Those killers will just work around him as soon as they find out that he's alone. You should be gettin' away from here as quick as you can. My mule's slowin' you down. Let me go and you can get clear away. That's the only chance you have left.'

The sheriff hoped that his prisoner was wrong but secretly felt that he could be right. However, he was not one to give way to his doubts. He had not intended for Marty to fight a sustained delaying action but the period of inter-mittent firing had continued for longer than he had envisaged.

'Shut your face and shake up that jackass, Brown, or whatever your name is. Marty's buying us time and I don't intend to waste it. If I find you're deliberately slowing me down, I'll shoot you.'

'You can't do that. It'd be murder.'

'Who's to know? Now get moving and remember, I have a fast horse here and if you try to run away I'll run you down and kill you.'

Cooper decided to save his breath. He urged the mule into a gallop, following the hoof tracks that led from Gopher Creek.

The distant gunshots were drowned out by the pounding of hoofs as the two riders urged their mounts along the rough trail. With their thoughts on the fighting behind them and their gaze on the ground ahead, they turned a bend in a narrow canyon. There, directly in their path, they saw a horseman looking at them down the barrel of a Henry repeater.

CHAPTER 14

Marty was thankful that he had selected a position where tree trunks and boulders offered good protection for himself and his horse. As long as he stayed where he was he could command the trail and give Bullseye and his prisoner a reasonable start. He had a fair view of the huge boulder that sheltered his enemies and, by their inaccurate fire, he knew that they had not pinpointed his exact position. Once he had seen by the gun smoke that a shot had been so badly aimed that it was simply a waste of ammunition.

Initially Marty thought that the apparently random shots were an attempt to draw his fire. It was another shot from around the other corner of the boulder that suddenly set him thinking.

The shooters seemed to be taking turns with a Winchester firing around the right corner of the rock and a different weapon – that he assumed was Thorpe's Spencer – firing from the left corner. Two men were doing all the shooting. Were they just holding his attention? Where was the third pursuer?

Bullseye was lifting his shotgun, hoping it was not too late, when he recognized the skinny rider on the tall black horse.

121

'Don't shoot,' the rider called urgently. 'I'm Sheriff Kelner.'

Harvey lowered his rifle.

'Hell, I know who *you* are,' he said sheepishly, 'but the first one I saw was your prisoner and for a second I thought I'd run into the wrong crowd. Luckily I saw you just in time.'

'Just in time for you,' Bullseye growled. 'It saved you a bellyfull of buckshot. What are you doing, creeping up on me like that?'

'I wasn't creeping; you walked right into me. I figured you might need some help. Where's Marty?'

'He's back along the trail delaying Thorpe and his crew to give me a start with this varmint. Listen close and you'll hear a few shots. I'll go back for him if you take this prisoner in.'

Harvey shook his head. 'I ain't had much practice with prisoners. You bring your man in and I'll give Marty a hand.'

'That might be best. Be careful though. If you don't hear shooting it could mean that Marty's on his way, or it could mean that they got him. If you meet anyone on the trail make sure you see them before they see you.'

A couple more shots were heard in the distance.

'Sounds like Marty's still holding them up,' Harvey observed as urged his mare forward.

'Don't be too sure,' Bullseye shouted after him. 'One of them shots we heard might have got him. Be careful.'

Where was the third shooter? Marty had no reason to believe that he had been put out of action in that first flurry of shots. He had seen three riders when he fired his warning shot but then they had scattered into the landscape so quickly that he'd had no time to seek out individuals.

From his elevated position on the slope he could see to his left front: on his side of the trail the old landslide had cleared a broad area on his right front. Chaparral had taken root there. It covered a wide strip of the disturbed area but it was only a couple of feet high. An attacker would really need to stand up to get a clear shot at him, but there was ample room to belly-crawl and work around his right flank. It was a big patch of dangerous ground and suddenly Marty realized that the third man would most likely be concealed there.

He had given Bullseye a long start; now he decided that it was time to go. He would fire another shot to advertise that he was still there, then he would creep back to his horse and ride away.

Sanderson was within thirty yards of Marty when the latter fired his last shot. He saw the grey gun-smoke as it spurted from the undergrowth covering a few irregular rocks. While intently seeking his target he saw movement among the bushes but could not shoot from his present position. He took a chance and jumped to his feet, throwing his rifle to his shoulder as he did so.

Out of the corner of his eye Marty saw the movement just as he was crouching, about to retreat. He knew that Thorpe could not see him but Sanderson's proximity came as a shock. A worse surprise came as he flicked the carbine's loading lever and squeezed the trigger, only to hear the firing pin fall on an empty chamber. He had not been counting his shots and had fired the eleven cartridges that the carbine carried when fully loaded. Already he saw Sanderson's rifle swinging towards him.

In desperation he reached for his big Colt and jumped sideways. He felt the wind of Sanderson's bullet.

The Colt was clear of the holster and fully cocked by the time Sanderson had reloaded his Winchester. Marty fought down the urge to fire as quickly as possible. A rifle was always more accurate than a pistol at the range between them. Marty knew that if he missed, his enemy was most unlikely to do the same. It seemed the longest fraction of a second he had ever experienced as he forced himself to align his sights on Sanderson's body. He was not aiming at any specific part, he just knew that he had to score a hit.

He did it even as he heard the roar of his opponent's rifle. Something buzzed past his shoulder and he caught a glimpse of his target reeling sideways and dropping his rifle. Sanderson was still awkwardly trying to draw a revolver as Marty took aim properly and knocked him off his feet with another well-placed shot.

Thorpe heard the flurry of shots. 'Sanderson's got him,' he shouted to Glasson, 'Come on.'

Both men ran from cover looking up the slope, ready to support their comrade.

While they were still on the trail looking to see what was happening a rifle shot, seemingly from nowhere, sent Glasson tumbling backwards.

With instincts honed by years on the outlaw trail Thorpe saw at a glance that the situation had suddenly been reversed.

He ran back under cover, unhitched his horse and threw himself into the saddle. His plans had been totally wrecked; now all that mattered was survival. Driving home the spurs, he fled into the sheltering trees.

CHAPTER 15

Marty heard Thorpe's horse galloping away but could not see it through the trees. His main interest was in Sanderson, who was stretched on the ground but still moving feebly. He checked first to make sure that his opponent was not holding a gun nor was in easy reach of one. Previous experience had taught him that even a dying man was dangerous if he got his hands on a gun.

He need not have worried though, because without saying a word Sanderson shuddered, went rigid for an instant, then relaxed completely in death.

Harvey remained mounted and seeing that Glasson was dead turned his horse up the slope.

'Are you OK?' he asked as he halted beside Marty.

'I'm fine. Didn't expect to see you here but I'm mighty glad you came. For a while it looked like I would be fighting all three of those skunks on my own.'

'Thorpe got away. I thought I should have gone after him but this leg is still too sore for hard riding. I forgot about it when I heard the shooting but it's letting me know it's there now.'

'Did you see Bullseye?'

'Yes, he was busy with a prisoner so I told him I'd help you out. You know, you shouldn't be allowed out without a keeper.'

'Do you reckon Thorpe will keep running?'

Harvey squirmed a little in his saddle. 'If he's got any sense he will,' he replied. 'He seems to have a serious shortage of partners at present. Let's head back to Gopher Creek and leave Bullseye to decide what he wants to do about all the bodies and the stuff that's scattered around these parts.'

'Good idea,' Marty agreed. 'Let's collect any guns and cartridge belts and take them with us. Bullseye would want them brought in. We can leave the rifles to be picked up later.'

Harvey began to unload his Henry rifle, placing the bullets in a pocket on his chaps.

'There's a nice new Winchester there, so I reckon I'll work a swap. I'm sure that our dear departed skunk here won't mind. We could make a few bucks out of selling some of the stuff we've collected here.'

Marty buckled two gun belts with three revolvers around his saddle horn.

'I don't reckon Bullseye would approve of that,' he told his friend. 'He's straight down the middle as far as the law is concerned. I've sounded him out about the mules but I have another idea in mind. One that he don't know about.'

Bullseye struggled for breath as he tried to loosen the dead man's arms from around his neck. Cooper had taken him by surprise, looping his cuffed hands over the sheriff's head and dragging the chain of the handcuffs tightly against his throat.

The attack came in an awkward place where both men's mounts were forced together by a rough piece of ground. Cooper's mule had halted and Bullseye came up beside it to see what was obstructing their progress.

The prisoner had obeyed all his orders and the tired lawman had let down his guard.

Suddenly Cooper launched himself from his mule and looped his arms around Bullseye's neck. The sudden movement startled their mounts, causing them to shy apart while the men fell to the ground between them. The prisoner was underneath when the pair hit the rocky ground and the fall hurt him, but in sheer desperation he maintained the pressure on his captor's throat.

Stunned and shocked, Bullseye knew that he could lose consciousness in a short while but he did not panic. His hand went to his revolver butt and twisted the weapon between himself and his prisoner after he had freed it from the holster. He pushed the muzzle against Cooper's body and fired the first shot.

A shout that could have been from pain or anger confirmed that the bullet had struck home but the sheriff had no chance to judge the severity of the wound. The pressure was still on his throat so he fired again. This time he felt a convulsive movement from his attacker and the handcuffs chain slackened.

Bullseye struggled out of the limp arms and rolled on to his side. He saw that Cooper was dead: his eyes and mouth both open in a shocked grimace and his shirt front smoldering from the close-range gun flash. The dead man's hat had fallen near by and the sheriff used it to beat out the small flame that was starting to take hold.

His throat was hurting and he knew that the unexpected physical strain would have him stiff and sore tomorrow. As he replaced the fired cartridges in his gun Bullseye spoke to the dead outlaw:

'You nearly got me, you sneaky son of a bitch. Serves me right for being careless.'

His horse and the mule were standing nervously near by, so the lawman caught them and secured both to a convenient tree. He had intended to load Cooper's body on to the mule but then found that he lacked the strength to do so. He could abandon the corpse and ride to town for assistance or he could wait for Harvey and Marty to join him – if that was possible.

A doubt continued to nag him. If the two cowhands had run into trouble the next people he saw could be Thorpe and his friends. Part of him said to leave Cooper and ride for town, but the lawman in him said that he should wait until he knew the fate of his two helpers.

It was a very nervous sheriff who took Cooper's gun and his shotgun and concealed himself beside the trail. At worst he could be facing three men and he might account for two if the ambush succeeded. The third man might run or fight and Bullseye hoped that he would take the former option. He was all too aware of the toll that passing years and wounds had taken on his body, his reflexes and his self-confidence.

From somewhere down the trail a horse snorted. The chill that ran down the lawman's spine seemed to dispel his doubts. It was too late to run. He cocked his shotgun, crouched lower in the concealing bushes and waited.

Anxiety turned to relief as he recognized the two cowhands.

The mountains behind Gopher Creek were throwing long shadows across the town when the grim procession arrived. Not many people were about because it was a weekday and the town's small businesses were preparing to close. Those who were in the street watched as Harvey and Bullseye rode ahead of Marty, who was leading the mule with Cooper's body draped across the saddle.

The sheriff was rubbing a sore neck and Harvey rode with his wounded leg unsupported by the stirrup.

A couple of children were herded back inside by their mother and a few drinkers from the saloon gathered in front of its entrance. One, more curious than the rest, even followed the procession along.

Marjie was putting clean sheets on a bed in a front

128

upstairs room at Mooney's hotel. She glanced out of the window just as she saw the group riding past below. With relief she recognized Marty, Harvey and Bullseye and wondered briefly about the identity of the dead man. No doubt she would find out later as Gopher Creek was too small to keep secrets about such serious events.

There was one more observer sitting on his horse at the end of the long straight street. Thorpe had doubled back on his tracks and followed the sheriff's party back to town. He had kept unobserved at a safe distance but at one point he had been close enough to see that the dead man was his former gang member.

Certainly he would tell no tales now, but had he lived long enough to disclose what he knew?

CHAPTER 16

Bullseye had arranged for Cooper's burial and completed the necessary paperwork. He was feeling his age and was considering closing the office for a quick nap in an empty cell when he heard boots and dragging spurs on the boardwalk outside.

He knew who was coming even before Marty and Harvey walked into his office. The latter was still limping slightly but was walking better than he had been the previous day.

'What are you pair up to?' the sheriff growled. He liked the two cowhands but had a carefully cultivated image of irascibility to preserve.

'We were wondering about something,' Harvey said.

'Well. spit it out. Don't beat around the bush.'

Marty spoke first. He mentioned the mules left by Thorpe's men after the fight at the creek and offered to bring them in. In return they would claim any unbranded animals and would also mark the sites of any bodies they found so that their burials could be arranged.

Harvey reminded him that there were four bodies needing attention, but one might prove difficult to find. For that reason himself and Marty would have the best chance of locating the missing corpse. They would mark the whereabouts of the remains for the gravediggers. Some of the country was impassable to wheeled vehicles, and when the work was done the belongings and tools would have to be brought by pack animals to a collection point before being transferred to a wagon.

The idea appealed to Bullseye but he did not want to appear too eager.

'What if them mules are wearing Mexican brands?' he asked. He had seen a Mexican brand on the mule that Cooper had been riding.

'Hell, Sheriff,' Marty objected, 'some of those Mex brands look like spider webs. No one can read them anyway. Are they legal this side of the border?'

'I suppose not, but I'll charge you a nominal amount if they have Mexican brands, so you have proof of legal ownership. There's one more condition. All deals are off if we find proper bills of sale for any American-branded stock. I'll go out with the Morlinas brothers with a wagon and team to pick up the pieces in the next day or so. I'll see you when you get back with whatever stock you can collect.'

Out in the street again Harvey and Marty were wondering which side had gotten the better of the agreement.

'I'm not sure we got the best deal here,' Marty said doubtfully. Harvey laughed.

'I reckon we'll still be a long way in front if this idea of mine works out.'

Thorpe was seething with anger as he returned to the scene of the latest fight and set about planning a completely new operation. His grand plan had been wrecked, his gang had been destroyed and soon he would be short of ready cash, an important commodity for a man on the run.

The mounts and equipment of his late gang were scattered around the area and he had no means of collecting or moving them, let alone arranging sales.

He found the horse and mule, still saddled and feeding on a grassy flat near by. They were no trouble to catch so he secured both, then rifled the saddlebags. They contained some spare ammunition that fitted neither his rifle nor his revolver and little else that he considered worth the trouble of carrying. Time was more important and survival depended upon moving quickly.

He discarded both saddles, took the bridle off the mule and turned it loose. The horse he would lead with him as a spare mount; it could be sold later.

By following the sheriff and the others to town Thorpe had learned a lot about the geography of the area, which he knew would offer many places of concealment. He would stay around the district, hoping to learn from local gossip if Cooper had revealed the location of the missing money before he died.

As he had never been to Gopher Creek before he knew that only the sheriff and the two cowboys were likely to recognize him. He was hoping to obtain a few supplies and possibly glean a bit of information provided he entered the town while his enemies were elsewhere.

Thorpe still had the spyglass that he had taken from Lane's body. From a bluff south of the town he could see straight down the main street. Knowing the locations of particular people would be vital to the plan he was mentally building.

CHAPTER 17

The delights of civilization, as represented by the town of Gopher Creek, quickly became boring for the Gilbert sisters. The pittance that their joint efforts earned at Mooney's hotel would never be enough for coach fares to any sizeable town where employment prospects were better.

It had been a busy day in the hotel laundry, washing bed sheets and pillow covers and then putting them through a large mangle that squeezed the water from the washing between heavy wooden rollers. The sisters took it in turns, with one cranking the handle of the mangle and the other carrying the wet washing in baskets to the clothes'line.

As they were pegging the last of the washing on the line Judy spoke.

'This isn't going to work,' she said. 'I can't see how we will ever make enough to get out of this town. If we had not been held up by that Indian scare we might have been able to reach a decent town and find proper work. We have a sewing machine but it looks as though we will never get to use it.'

Marjie put the final peg in the last sheet and picked up the empty clothes basket.

'Sewing machines are rare out here,' she replied, 'and the one we have will pay for itself if we can only get to a reasonably sized town. We only have two trunks and the

machine is in a box; maybe we could find a friendly team-
ster who would take us. I would not care if we had to walk
beside an ox team – just to get out of this hole in the
ground. Marty and Harvey have the right idea with riding
horses and a pack animal but we could not afford an outfit
like they have.'

'You forgot to mention, sis, that they are also armed to
the teeth and not everyone around here is friendly. We not
only need a form of transport, we need some sort of an
escort.'

'At least we are getting room and meals here,' Marjie
said in an effort to be positive about their futures.

'Folks in jail get that,' Judy reminded her.

Marty and Harvey left their camp just on sunrise. If all went
according to plan they had a long day ahead of them. As
their horses walked briskly in the fresh morning air Harvey
looked at the rough country ahead.

'You know, Marty, I'd be a hellova lot happier if I knew
where Thorpe was. I ain't sure that letting him get away yesterday was such a good idea. He could be waiting along
here somewhere just to ambush us.'

'That's possible, but I was talking to Bullseye last night
when you were feeding the horses. He reckoned that we did
the right thing. He found an old reward poster for
Thornhill or Thorpe or whoever he really is.

'It appears that he was one of Quantrill's men, and a
mighty dangerous one at that. According to Bullseye a lot
of them were what folks used to call "revolver fighters".
Because the old cap-and-ball six-shooters were so slow to
load, these characters carried as many as four of them. They
often had a couple more in holsters on their saddles and
could shoot as well from horseback as they could standing
on their own two feet.

'He reckons there's not much to worry about though,

because Thorpe would be heading back to where he would have friends. His stamping ground was a long way east of here; there's no reason for him to hang about these parts.'

'What if he's looking for that watch?'

Marty had to admit that his tall friend had a point. After that there was little conversation and both paid close attention to the scenery around them.

An hour's ride took the pair to the site of their last skirmish. The two dead bodies were undisturbed by scavenging animals but the tracks on the ground and the abandoned saddles showed that someone else had been at the site ahead of them, and not too long ago. Marty pointed to a hoofprint in the soft soil of the trail.

'I reckon that's the track of that big brown horse that Thorpe rides. Your Emma might be nearly as tall but her feet ain't that big.'

Harvey looked uneasily about them. 'Ain't it nice to know that that murdering sonofabitch is lurking around here somewhere,' he replied.

'He could be on the run,' Marty suggested. 'Them saddles he left were worth good money. If he wasn't in such an all-fired hurry he could have taken them and his side-kicks' mounts to sell later on.'

'Maybe, but look around. He took the saddle blankets. My guess is that he intends to set up a camp around here. He seems determined to get back that watch. Darned if I know why.'

'No watch is worth getting killed over. There must be something else.'

'He could be out for revenge,' Harvey speculated.

The sun climbed higher and with daylight they saw buzzards circling in the cloudless blue sky. It was also apparent that there were two separate flocks of the scavengers; one to the south-east and the other across the ridge to the south-west.

Marty stood in his stirrups and surveyed the landscape before pointing to the ridge on their right.

'I reckon we might find the fella Thorpe chased away if we look over there first. The loose mules will be hanging around the grass and water where that other gunman was shot, so we won't disturb them just yet.'

'Suits me,' Harvey agreed. 'If we find that *hombre*, we can save time for Bullseye and his helpers and he might be a bit more generous with any deals we do with the mules. There's something else too. Everyone seems to have forgotten about the harness that was dumped with the wagon. That could be worth a buck or two if it's any good.'

'I wonder what Bullseye would think of a deal like that.'

'What he don't know won't hurt him. There are no brands on harness and just look over to the north. There's big clouds building up and a storm looks likely. A heap of rain will run into that gully and whatever is left there will be buried in mud or washed away.'

'We can't let good harness go to waste,' Marty said after a long glance at the darkening sky.

Agreeing upon their plan, the two cowboys crossed the ridge. As they had expected, they quickly found what the scavengers had left of the missing man.

It did not take long to collect a few big stones and pile them in a heap at the lip of the washout to show where the last of the 'cholera victims' rested. With great difficulty Harvey struggled back onto Emma.

'We need to have a look at that wrecked wagon and be back in this area when Bullseye and his helpers arrive,' he observed.

'We need to remember too that Thorpe is still around here somewhere,' Marty warned. 'If we keep to open country as much as possible there's less chance of us being ambushed.'

The ride took a bit longer by a safer course, but within

half an hour they halted at the gully where the wrecked wagon rested on its side.

As Harvey was still handicapped by his wounded leg Marty left him to keep watch while he climbed down to the wagon. On hands and knees he crawled under the slack canvas that had been the wagon's cover and found what he sought.

The harness was in a tangle but seemed to be all there except for some of the bridles that the men had taken when they took to their saddles. The canvas cover had protected the harness from the weather but it would be of little use if heavy rain should flood the ravine. A glance at the sky showed that rain was a distinct possibility.

Dark clouds were drifting in from the north so the pair set to work. Marty released the tie strings on the wagon cover, pulled it clear of the other debris and started throwing the harness into its center. Then he pulled all the corners together and secured them with a piece of rope that he had salvaged. Harvey threw down a lariat and Marty attached it to the top of the large bundle. The other end of the rope he fastened to his saddle horn.

'Haul away,' Marty called.

Harvey started Emma backing and the bundle rose in jerks until it finally rolled over the edge of the gully.

Marty climbed back to the level ground and rolled the bundle onto a sheet of rock that was protruding a few inches above the surface of the plain. Satisfied that the harness was protected from any rain or run-off water, he mounted Lonesome and together the partners rode back to where they were to meet Bullseye.

The sheriff was watching two large Mexicans fill in a grave where the remains of Kirk had been hastily interred. The lawman gave the newcomers a sour look.

'I wondered where you two had gotten to,' he growled.

'We've been looking around,' Harvey explained.

'Thorpe's most likely around here somewhere.'

'He ain't that stupid. I got a telegraph message after you snuck out this morning. It seems there was a bank robbery at Cedar Flat and around twenty thousand dollars, give or take a thousand or two, was taken. The news was delayed by the recent break in the line.'

Harvey's face reflected his sudden concern. 'So where does that leave us? Are we still suspected bank robbers?'

'You don't need to worry. Thorpe is now wanted for that. He talked his way into the marshal's job and robbing the bank was his long-term plan.'

'So he could be that Thornhill character?' Marty asked.

'Could be.'

'If he has all that money why is he chasing us about a forty-dollar watch?' Harvey wondered.

'I don't have all the details but, according to a member of Thorpe's criminal organization, there was a double-cross of some kind and the money was stolen again before Thorpe could get his thieving hands on it. Seems that a minor member of the gang was picked up in Kansas for horse-stealing and he spilled his guts trying to avoid a necktie party. That's all I know, but the regular mail is running again and I'll get more details soon.'

The two Mexicans had finished their task and joined the others after drinking deeply from a water canteen.

The Morlinas brothers, Pedro and Luis, were big, bearded men in their thirties, clad in buckskin pants and faded red undershirts. Both wore the moccasins favoured by mountain trappers, and their gun belts, each with a holstered revolver and Bowie knife attached, lay close at hand to where they had been working. They were fanning themselves with their large straw sombreros when the sheriff introduced them to the others.

'Meet the Morlinas brothers. The one on your left is Pedro and the feller on your right is Luis. They're the best workers in Gopher Creek and I always call on them when I need some help. With Thorpe somewhere around, they could be mighty handy.'

Introductions followed complete with crushing hand-shakes from the two brothers; then Bullseye switched back to business.

'Have you pair found our next customer?'

'We have,' Harvey replied. 'As soon as Pedro and Luis put their tools on the pack mule we will take you to where he is. Then we'll round up those loose mules and take them back to Gopher Creek with us. There should be five of them here somewhere.'

Marty pointed towards the ridge. 'I can see two up there, feeding near the timber. The others won't be far away.'

'Could be they're enjoying life and might not want to come back to work,' Bullseye told them.

'We've both herded mules before,' Harvey said dismissively. 'We'll get 'em. They're easy to handle, if you know how.'

'I never liked mules,' the sheriff muttered. Luis took the long ear of the pack mule.

'Don't take any notice of that *hombre*, Dolores,' he said in a stage whisper. 'He is in a bad mood today.'

The party crossed the ridge and buzzards showed the location of the last corpse. While Bullseye and his assistants were busy with its burial Harvey and Marty went back over the ridge in search of the mules. Once collected the animals would be held until the sheriff's party rejoined them. With the shadow of Thorpe over the scene all would return together for safety's sake.

The mules had moved closer to the creek and all five were now there. They stopped feeding and moved uneasily at the riders' approach.

'I'll go a bit wide of them,' Marty said. He unhitched his lariat and shook out a loop. 'If they make a break they'll probably come this way. I have Chief's bell in my saddle-bag. I'll put it on the first one I catch and when I lead it away the others will come out and follow. It's an old trick but works well.'

His eyes were on the mules as he rode through a patch of high sage.

Uncharacteristically, Lonesome shied. After readjusting his balance Marty saw what had startled the horse. An upturned pack saddle was lying half-concealed among the bushes.

The mules could wait. He called to Harvey and dismounted to inspect what he had found.

Just then Bullseye and the Morlinas brothers appeared over the distant ridge. Marty called to them and waved his hat.

CHAPTER 18

Marty had opened the pack thinking that one of the grain bags might be useful for carrying the salvaged harness. Immediately the weight and the clinking of coins told him what the bag contained. A similar result occurred when he moved the second sack. The others came at a gallop, expecting that he had found another body.

'What's so all-fired urgent?' Bullseye demanded as they reined in. Marty pointed to the pack spread out among the sage.

'I think I've found that stolen bank money.'

An hour before sundown the storm broke. The thunder had been rumbling for much of the afternoon, gradually drawing closer to Gopher Creek. A howling wind came first and then a burst of torrential rain with jagged lightning ripping across the dark sky.

Those who could sought shelter among the buildings, keeping away from wildly lashing trees because of the danger of falling branches or lightning strikes. Some, caught away from shelter, could only don slickers – if they had them, while those travellers caught without any rain protection could only look forward to a cold, very wet night.

The weather suited Thorpe perfectly. Wearing a long

141

yellow slicker with the collar turned up and a sodden hat pulled low over his eyes, he looked no different from anyone else in town. As a stranger there was minimal chance that anyone would recognize him, and from his vantage point he had seen Bullseye leave town that morning.

He placed his horse under shelter at the local livery barn. For a dollar he could get it a good feed and, being under cover, his saddle would be kept dry. Thorpe would go to great lengths to avoid a long ride in a wet saddle.

Before leaving the barn he took an empty flour sack from a saddlebag, folded it and placed it in a big side pocket of his slicker. As a precaution he removed one of his revolvers from its holster and placed it in the other outside pocket.

His next stop was at the town's only general store, where he bought two pounds of bacon and a couple of cans of sardines. A cardboard carton of cracker biscuits completed his order. With his purchases in the flour bag he hurried next door to where a bakery was about to close for the night.

The sight and smell of freshly baked bread set Thorpe's mouth watering and he bought two loaves which also went into his sack. He was hungry and had to resist the temptation to tear the bread apart with his bare hands and start eating, but such behaviour could draw attention to him. His survival depended upon being as inconspicuous as possible.

A quick visit to the saloon followed. Few customers had ventured out in the wild weather. With nobody to pay him any attention, he had one quick drink, bought a bottle of whiskey to take with him and left.

The bartender had not been very talkative but he did disclose that the sheriff was investigating some recent shootings; however, in his absence there were no details.

He found a small Mexican restaurant with a limited menu. Food more to his taste might have been available at the saloon kitchen but the risk of discovery was greater there. He was happy to settle for beans and chili washed down with coffee.

Just as he was finishing his meal Thorpe glanced out through the window in time to see five horsemen riding past, with two pack mules being led and four others being loose-herded behind. Two of the riders were Mexicans looking miserable in sodden ponchos, while the others were wrapped in slickers. Although their features were hidden Thorpe knew their identities and decided to linger in the town a little longer. If something important had happened, the word would soon spread.

When he left the restaurant Thorpe sheltered under the awning of the general store which by then had closed for the night. The lamps along the street were few and far between and the shadowy patches along the boardwalk enabled him to get fairly close to the unfolding scene without being noticed.

The two cowboys, on Bullseye's instruction, had remained mounted with their carbines in hand. One of the Mexicans was helping the sheriff remove the pack saddle and carried it into the building. The other Mexican waited for the gear to be removed, then herded the mule with the others to a corral behind the jail.

A dozen people were a crowd in Gopher Creek and they were far from quiet as they asked many questions, mostly all at once. With the pack safely inside, Bullseye appeared at his office door.

'You can all go home,' he shouted. 'There's nothing to see here. My men and I are tired. I'll answer any questions tomorrow morning. There's nothing to worry about.'

A voice from somewhere in the crowd challenged that statement.

'Why have you got armed guards out here if you don't need them?'

'They're from Texas and they ain't got sense enough to come in out of the rain.'

Thorpe knew from past experience that the two men on their horses were far from the dumb cowhands that the sheriff had implied they were. There was something very important in that pack.

Suddenly he guessed what it was.

The storm had cleared away by sunrise the next morning and Marty and Harvey were surveying the wreckage of their camp. The tent had been torn down and their blankets and few belongings were a sodden mess. They had seen the damage as they entered the town but had taken up Bullseye's offer of dry accommdation in the empty jail cells. Now, after a hasty breakfast at the sheriff's expense, they had returned to their camp to salvage what they could.

They were hanging their blankets from tree branches and draping mud-stained spare clothing over nearby bushes.

'I reckon we'll need more than that little tent when we get to Montana,' Marty muttered. 'If stories are right, it can get mighty cold up there.'

Harvey pointed to a light wagon resembling a military ambulance that was parked on vacant ground beside the sheriff's office.

'That's what we need. A couple of mules could pull it easily. I counted three mules among those we brought in last night that we should be able to buy if Bullseye keeps his word. We could get the harness that we saved. Nobody will be looking for it after that storm last night. The wreckage of the wagon will be all washed away or half-buried by mud, but that canvas cover should have protected the harness we kept out of the weather. We could take turns in driving and we could sleep dry every night.'

144

Both agreed that the wagon would be ideal for their purposes but their finances were limited. They would seek out the vehicle's owner and determine whether they could pay the asking price.

Marjie's shoulders drooped and disappointment showed on her pretty face. She had been watching as Judy calculated their finances on a sheet of paper. She knew without asking that their lack of funds would keep them stuck in Gopher Creek.

'It looks as though we won't make it to Virginia City.' Judy was trying hard to keep the disappointment from her voice. 'We have a great sewing machine but there will never be enough work for us around here. If we sold the machine we might get the fare to Montana, but sewing by hand would never give us the output to make our business a success.'

With an enthusiasm that she did not feel, Marjie tried to be positive.

'Don't worry, sis. Maybe something will come up. I suppose Marty and Harvey will be on their way soon. It would be nice to catch up with them some time in the future.'

CHAPTER 19

A week had passed since the discovery of the money. It had totalled fifteen thousand and twenty-six dollars and forty cents, considerably less than the first reports had suggested. Bullseye had insisted that it should be counted twice and then held securely in a locked cell. Marty and Harvey together with the Morlinas brothers were recruited to guard the money in twenty-four-hour shifts until heavily armed express messengers arrived to take it back to its rightful owners.

Although the cowboys were sick of Gopher Creek the sheriff had kept them on the payroll until the whole transaction had been formalized. Two dollars each per day was a welcome replenishment to their funds. In addition, Bullseye said that the bank was authorizing a reward to be split evenly between those who had recovered the money. He warned that it would not be a large amount but said that he would give them a good deal on any of the mules that had no evidence of ownership. It would be worth their while to wait around until the financial matters were settled.

They were seeing more of the Gilbert sisters in the little spare time that both parties had. After spending so much of their time in rough camps Marty and Harvey were starting to enjoy the feminine company. Suddenly Gopher Creek was not as dull as they had imagined it to be.

Harvey's wounded leg was still sore; recent long hours in the saddle had slowed the healing process but it did give him something to discuss with Judy, who seemed to have made his return to health her personal project.

'You're a sneaking polecat,' Marty teased him. 'I might have to get you to shoot me in the leg so that I can get Marjie to look after me.'

'We're just friends,' Harvey protested. 'I don't intend letting any girl stop me getting to Montana.'

'Just remember that,' Marty admonished.

Secretly he was growing fond of Marjie. She was bright company, quick to laugh, gentle and considerate. If he was the marrying type, Marty told himself, she was the girl he would choose, but he would not expect any girl to wait for him while he was roaming around seeing new country. He liked his life just the way it was – or so he kept telling himself.

Thorpe had seen the heavily guarded special coach that had taken the stolen money back to Cedar Flats and had no intention of committing suicide with a single-handed holdup attempt. The money was gone and he would soon be headed for other parts but he had given himself one more task. He would reclaim Sutcliffe's watch and square accounts with the two drifters who had caused him so much trouble.

In true guerilla fashion he was living off the land. From various vantage points he watched the road through Gopher Creek. His base was a well-hidden makeshift camp with its few comforts forcibly acquired from the pack of a single traveller. One shot, fired from concealment, had killed the unsuspecting stranger. Quickly Thorpe had caught the man's pony and pack horse. He had slung the dead man across the saddle and led the animals into the mountain brush, where he plundered the body before concealing it.

His next move was to unsaddle the animals and turn them loose. He had already decided against keeping a spare horse and had let go Glasson's mount with the others. They would wander back to familiar territory, just some of the many straying animals that travellers often encountered on Western trails. The food supplies from the pack, when augmented with game animals, would last for a considerable time. If they did not Thorpe knew that other potential victims would already be on the trail because it eventually led to the goldfields many miles to the north.

The two cowhands had rebuilt their camp near the creek, where there was plenty of long, lush grass on which to stake out their horses. From one of his hidden observation points Thorpe could see their horses through his telescope: Harvey's distinctive black mare was easy to recognize. Thorpe knew that while he could see the horses his intended victims were still in the town.

A couple of days passed, then Bullseye sent for Marty and Harvey. The Cedar Flat bank had telegraphed through five separate payments, each of one hundred dollars, for the party that had recovered the lost money.

As he handed the two their shares and received receipts in return, the sheriff was angrily casting doubts on the legitimacy of the bank's directors' decision. He felt that the reward should have been greater.

Harvey took advantage of the situation and broached the subject of the mules they had also recovered. Three had indecipherable Mexican brands that constituted no real evidence of ownership.

'We didn't get much for our efforts,' Harvey complained to the sheriff. 'Will you keep your word about those mules?

There's three that don't have identifiable American brands. If we can still get them at a good price it would make up for those miserable bankers short-changing us.'

'I'll keep my word. Any money raised will only go to the town council so I'm not wanting to make a profit for myself. In appreciation for your help you can have the three with no proof of ownership for ten dollars a head. I'll give you a proper receipt in case someone thinks you might have stolen them.'

Marty and Harvey knew that each mule was worth about sixty dollars in a sale ring; they accepted the offer quickly in case Bullseye should change his mind. Gradually their plan was coming together.

The wagon had proved to be a bit light and a bit small for heavy freighting; its owner had left it with the saloon keeper to settle his account after a week of heavy drinking and gambling.

Bert Ross, the new owner, had found the vehicle difficult to sell. He jumped at the opportunity when Harvey offered to take it off his hands for seventy dollars. The tubby little saloon owner knew that he would turn a modest profit on the deal while getting get rid of what he considered to be a white elephant.

The next day the two cowhands left town before sunrise with their newly acquired mules and brought back the harness and cover they had salvaged from the wrecked wagon. The canopy would be a trifle large for their wagon but would suffice to put over the existing one when cold weather hit. They had been warned that double canvas was necessary in Montana winters.

They had a team of two mules and a spare one that they could use if necessary or sell later. They also planned to sell Chief when they reached a place where horse prices were higher.

'Just think of it,' Marty said. 'We can travel in style, carry all we need and sleep warm and dry every night. No more living out of saddlebags and packs.'

'It looks as though the boys will be leaving soon.' Marjie tried to keep the regret and disappointment out of her voice. 'I looked out of the window a while ago and Harvey was driving past with a pair of mules drawing a wagon. It looked as though he was trying them out.'

Judy lifted the flatiron from the stove top and decided it was hot enough to start ironing tablecloths.

'Yes,' she replied, 'Marty told me yesterday that they would use a wagon on the way to Virginia City. If the idea doesn't work out, they can sell it there. I wonder if we could stow away?'

'If only we could get to Virginia City we could soon make money with our sewing machine. But the journey is still too dangerous for ladies travelling unescorted. I was talking to Rebecca Peters yesterday and she said that she and her family were going there too, but they were waiting to join up with a few more travellers. There are still scattered Indian raids and road agents are robbing – and sometimes murdering, too.'

'Who is Rebecca Peters?' Judy asked between swipes with the iron.

'I met her yesterday at the store. She seems very nice. She and her husband Sean and their young daughter are travelling in a wagon. They're both schoolteachers and are going to help set up a school in Montana. They call their daughter Georgia or Georgina – something like that.

'They're going to a place called Helena, to go into partnership there with some teacher named Egan with high hopes for setting up a top-class school. Rebecca says that Helena is going to grow quickly. It might be a good place for us to go into business.'

'From what I have heard the trail to Montana is reckoned to be very dangerous,' Judy said. 'For safety's sake they should join up with Harvey and Marty. Those two would be very good escorts.'

'Don't I know it,'Marjie said wistfully.

Because it was before dawn Thorpe had missed seeing the two cowhands when they left the town to retrieve the harness. When his telescope failed to find the horses at their usual grazing his immediate impression was that the pair might not be intending to return.

At first he felt that he should saddle his horse and pursue them, but then he saw that their tent was still standing and their pinto pack horse was picketed near by in a good patch of grass. Satisfied that his intended victims would be back, Thorpe settled down to wait.

CHAPTER 20

'We have to talk about them Gilbert girls,' Marty told Harvey. 'They're in a bad fix.'

'I know, but what can we do about it?'

'We can take them to Montana with us and drop them off in Virginia City. Marjie told me that they might get work there with one of them new sewing machines they got.'

'I suppose you know that Virginia City ain't a real city. There's only a couple of hundred people in the whole place. That might be fine from a ranching point of view but them girls wouldn't find much work there.'

'That don't matter; they need to get out of here. On our way north we're sure to pass a couple of big towns where they could set up a business. They could decide where they want to stay.'

Harvey pushed back his hat and scratched his head.

'You're loco,' he told his partner. 'Them girls are respectable. They can't be travelling alone with a pair like us.'

'They won't be alone with us. Don't forget that Sean Peters and his family will be with us. They can act as chaperones. They're both schoolteachers and you don't find anyone more respectable than that.'

'What about old Mudguts McGee who taught us reading and writing at Dry Creek? He couldn't teach hogs to be dirty and was drunk half the time.'

'He was an exception. We could fit the girls and their luggage in the wagon and they could sleep there. We could make do with the tent until we drop them off where they want to stay. It's only for a few weeks.'

Harvey thought for a while, then smiled. 'Maybe that ain't such a bad idea. I reckon they'd be real good company. But what if they don't want to travel with us?'

Harvey's doubts proved to be groundless. Judy and Marjie saw their offer as the answer to their many prayers.

Clementine Mooney was not exactly thrilled by losing two good workers at short notice but she knew the situation and did not press the sisters to stay.

Next morning the rising sun shed its light on a scene of feverish activity. Harvey was harnessing the wagon team while the sisters crammed their belongings into a single trunk each. Sean Peters easily lifted the heavy trunks into the back of the wagon, where Marty arranged them for transporting while allowing easy access to them. The much-prized sewing machine came next in its case, followed by assorted clothing and bedding and a readily accessible supply of food for that day. Finally, Marty squeezed in the pack that Chief had formerly carried. The pony and Harvey's saddled mare would be tethered to the wagon's tailboard while the Peters family hitched the spare mule to the tail of their wagon.

Harvey would ride in the wagon until the team had settled down and the sisters became proficient drivers.

The Peters family were all aboard when Marty mounted Lonesome and rode up to where they were holding their restless team.

'Do you have a gun?" he asked Sean.

'I don't carry a sidearm in my line of work,' the teacher admitted, 'but I have a shotgun and a repeating rifle for hunting purposes.'

'You'd best keep them and a supply of ammunition handy. If bad trouble comes you might need them in a hurry. Harvey and I will take turns of scouting ahead for any nasty surprises. I don't want to sound pessimistic, but not everyone we meet on the trail could have friendly intentions.'

Rebecca brushed back her blonde hair and tightened the chinstrap on her broad-brimmed hat.

'We've been on the trail for a long time and all three of us can shoot, but let's hope it never becomes necessary.'

'So do I,' Marty said. He turned Lonesome back to where Harvey had started his wagon rolling.

Sean released the brake, shook the reins and called to his four-mule team. The mules leaned into their collars and the wagon moved off at a lively walking pace.

Marty reined up beside their wagon where Harvey was sharing the driver's seat with the two sisters.

'I hope you ladies are learning all the right cuss words. You'll never be mule-skinners till you can cuss properly.'

Marjie laughed. 'Sean Peters started his team with just a few quiet words.'

'That's what a good education does for you,' Harvey replied. 'He can cuss in Latin or Greek and nobody knows what he's saying.'

'How did he teach the mules those languages?' Judy joined in the joke.

'That's something you need to ask him,' Harvey answered and immediately changed the subject.

Thorpe slammed shut his telescope and climbed down from the boulder that had given him a good view of the town. He had seen the wagons moving with Harvey's black horse tied behind the smaller one. His intended victims were leaving town, moving away from the safety provided by the law's presence. Now he would strike.

The wagons had a half-mile start on him but they were moving slowly. He could quickly reduce the distance between him and his intended prey by riding directly through the town. It was early morning with few people about, so the odds against being recognized made the gamble worth taking. He would strike a few miles beyond the town, where the gunshots were unlikely to be heard.

He wasted no time in reaching Gopher Creek but reluctantly slowed his horse in case he attracted undue attention. Seething as he was with thoughts of revenge, the brisk walk of his horse was still too slow a pace for Thorpe's liking. Halfway through the town he increased the pace to a trot. The wagons could not outrun him; once they were in sight he would begin stalking the travellers.

Their tracks showed plainly on the dusty trail and were easy to follow. Thorpe guessed that he was outnumbered by at least three to one but he was counting on the element of surprise and his extensive gunfighting experience to tip the scales in his favour. He was confident that if he planned properly he could account for two opponents before they became aware of the ambush.

Marty had scouted half a mile ahead of the wagons but had seen no fresh sign on the road. If anyone intended to waylay them they would need to stick to the regular trail because the country was rough on either side and the dirt road would show their tracks.

He turned Lonesome and cantered back to where the Peters wagon was just rounding a bend in the trail.

'The way looks clear in front,' he called to Sean. 'I'll just check now that nobody's coming up behind us.'

He had already given the same message to Harvey as he rode past. Harvey was more content to stay in the wagon because riding still made his wounded leg painful.

'Why is he looking behind us?' Marjie asked.

'Back in Texas we took part in posses chasing Comanche

and Kiowa raiders,' Harvey explained. 'They were hard to catch even when they left a clear trail. They could see if we were catching up to them because they guarded their back-trail as well as their front.

'Marty and me have always reckoned that was a smart thing to do. If someone is after your hide, it pays to watch both front and back.'

'And you think someone might be after your hide?' Marjie asked.

'Maybe. That Thorpe character could still be hanging around, or there could be road agents, even a Sioux or Cheyenne war party. It's best not to take chances.'

Marty rode back along the trail that snaked through a long canyon, the sides of which offered little concealment, but bends in the road prevented him from seeing far ahead.

Thorpe was approaching the same bend from the oppo-site direction. They were about a hundred yards apart when they rounded the corner and saw each other.

Recognition was mutual and both reacted instantly, spurring their horses forward and instinctively drawing revolvers. There could only be one winner.

Marty fired his first shot at long pistol-range. He had little chance of scoring a hit but needed to warn his friends.

Thorpe took scant notice of what he considered was a sign of panic and a wasted shot. With a revolver in his right hand he steered his big horse on a course intended to close with his opponent's mount on his right side.

The horses of the two antagonists appeared to be almost on a collision course. Thorpe raised his Colt to shoot at a range where a hit was almost certain. Just as he sighted along the barrel Marty's horse suddenly changed its direc-tion.

Steered by his rider, Lonesome cut across the front of Thorpe's horse, missing a collision by the narrowest of margins to gallop down the left side. The brown horse's sudden check almost unseated its rider and the outlaw had to switch his gun over his horse's neck and his bridle hand and twist in his saddle before he could take his shot.

With both horses galloping in opposite directions, Marty knew that his trained cutting horse could stop and turn back more quickly than the big brown, enabling him to position himself to aim at a mounted opponent's most vulnerable spot. Lonesome, through the feel of the bit, knew what was coming. The other horse did not and slowed considerably before it could be turned around.

Spinning on his hind legs, the cutting horse completed the hundred-and-eighty-degree manoeuvre while Thorpe's mount was only beginning its turn to the left. In a couple of strides Lonesome was in close range.

Thorpe threw an awkward shot in the hope that it might at least frighten Marty off, though he knew that the chance of scoring a hit was minimal.

Marty had no intention of losing the advantage because he suspected that Thorpe was probably a better hand with a gun. Lonesome was the more responsive and nimbler horse and, at his rider's directions, he held his place near the other animal's near-side quarter.

Marty snapped a close-range shot at Thorpe. He saw the big man twist in his saddle and drop his reins as the bullet tore through his left forearm. One rein fell onto the horse's neck but the other fell out of the rider's reach.

With all control of his thoroughly excited horse lost, Thorpe knew that Marty would be unlikely to miss with his next bullet. Thinking quickly, he threw away his gun and raised his empty right hand.

'I surrender,' he shouted. 'Don't shoot.'

Marty positioned Lonesome beside the brown and held his revolver only a couple of feet from its rider.

'Stop that horse or I'll shoot you off it.'

'I can't,' Thorpe said urgently. 'My arm's busted and I've dropped a rein. Don't shoot.'

Marty leaned over, lifted the revolver from Thorpe's left holster and threw it on the ground near the weapon that the outlaw had discarded. Then he holstered his own gun and leaned down to catch the dangling rein.

A rifle cracked, something buzzed past his ear and Marty heard a gasp from Thorpe. As the outlaw toppled from his saddle Harvey came racing up, a smoking Winchester still in his right hand.

The lanky cowboy reined in Emma in a shower of dust. He looked briefly at the dead man on the ground.

'Got him,' he said, with no small amount of satisfaction.

'Why did you shoot him, Harvey? He was surrendering.'

'He was about to put a window in your thick skull. Remember what Bullseye said about them old revolver fighters carrying extra pistols on their horses? That sneaky sonofabitch had a short-barrelled gun hanging in a holster under his lariat. You can see it just to the left of where he's lying. I heard the shooting and got here *pronto*. Looks like I was just in time.'

'You were at that,' Marty admitted. Any further conversation was halted by a call from Sean.

'Riders coming – three of them.'

The teacher had positioned himself on some rising ground at the bend so that he could see in both directions. He levered a bullet into the breech of his Winchester and took a sight on the approaching horsemen.

'Don't shoot,' Marty called. 'That's Bullseye and the Morlinas brothers.'

The sheriff was relieved to see that the travellers had sustained no injuries. He explained that he had seen Thorpe hurrying through town and consequently had collected his helpers before starting on the outlaw's tracks.

Bullseye dismounted and closely examined the body on the ground. He was checking various physical characteristics against a paper that he took from his pocket. Eventually he confirmed what he had suspected.

'Sure enough, this here Thorpe character is really Thornhill, the old Missouri guerilla. He was reckoned to be mighty good with a gun. If stories are right, he should have eaten both of you for breakfast.'

'Maybe he would have if we had met on foot,' Marty explained, 'but Lonesome here beat his horse with good footwork and Harvey finished him before he had a chance to play any more tricks.'

The sheriff shook his head at the gunman's downfall, then continued:

'There's still a reward, although it won't be a big one and it might take a while to collect it.'

'We ain't bounty hunters,' Harvey declared. 'Time is money and we can't afford to stay around. We need to be in Helena before the winter arrives.'

'I'll make the claim for you,' the sheriff said, 'and send all the details to you care of the post office in Helena. You have a long way to go and a bit of extra money might come in handy.' He paused a while, then added, 'Of course, you could always find ranch work around here. What's so special about Montana? It has outlaws, a heap of warlike Sioux, and a mighty cold climate. Do you really expect to make your fortunes there?'

'We don't expect to make fortunes,' Marty replied. 'For us it's just somewhere new but it's new starts for the Peters family and the Gilbert girls. They could make a difference to the place.'

'Time we were moving,' Harvey said. 'I'll drive the wagon for a few days until my leg gets right and both ladies can handle the mules.'

'Good luck to you all.' Bullseye chuckled, allowing

himself a rare smile. 'You're crazy, but if I was thirty years younger, I'd go with you. I might even chase one of those girls till she catches me.'

Marty turned to Harvey.

'You know, that mightn't be such a bad idea.'